THE LAST SWEET SONG
OF HAMMER DYLAN

A NASHVILLE P.I. SERIES

ROBERT J. RANDISI

WOLFPACK
PUBLISHING
— EST 2013 —

Copyright © 2019 Robert J. Randisi
All rights reserved.

Published in the United States by Wolfpack Publishing, Las Vegas.

Wolfpack Publishing
6032 Wheat Penny Avenue
Las Vegas, NV 89122

wolfpackpublishing.com

Paperback ISBN 978-1-64119-901-8
Ebook ISBN 978-1-64119-900-1

Library of Congress Control Number: 2019936120

THE LAST SWEET SONG
OF HAMMER DYLAN

PROLOGUE

OUTLAW COUNTRY MUSIC had been making a come-back for some time, now. Well, maybe not a comeback. One of the country music magazines did a story on it a while back, calling it a "resurgence."

Outlaw Country made its first appearance during the 60's, and became most popular during the 70's and, to some degree, the early 80's. You've heard of most of the big name "Outlaws," like Johnny Cash, Waylon Jennings, Merle Haggard, Willie Nelson, Kris Kristofferson, Hank Williams Jr., Leon Russell and others. Some of them, like Cash and Nelson, crossed over with their success to the pop charts. There were even some female outlaws who had crossover success of their own, like Jessi Colter with "I'm Not Lisa," and Tanya Tucker, most notably with "Delta Dawn."

The roots of Outlaw Country can even be traced to the 50's, and the music of Elvis Presley.

But there's a man who might have become the greatest Outlaw Country Artist of all time, if he hadn't pulled a disappearing act right at the height of his popularity. His first album went double platinum in 1972, and yielded four number one songs, two of which not only crossed over to the pop charts, but hit #1. He appeared on the *Glen Campbell Goodtime Hour, The Sonny and Cher Comedy Hour, The Dean Martin* Show and the *Tonight Show*, where Johnny Carson later said trying to interview him was like pulling teeth. Then, when he suddenly cancelled an appearance on *The Carol Burnett Show*, the search was on, but nobody could find him. Not his agent, not the members of his band, not his fiancé, not his record label . . . no one.

For a while, people thought he'd been kidnapped, but in the end it was decided that Hammer Dylan had pulled a disappearing act.

Gone and eventually forgotten.

Until now . . .

CHAPTER 1

I GOT an urgent call from Blake Shelton that he needed a guitar player for *The Voice* finale. He was performing a song with his remaining contestant, and his guitar player had come up sick. Could I fly to Culver City right away? I told him I'd be on the next plane. We didn't even discuss payment. I knew he'd pay me, but the amount didn't matter. I'd play for Blake for free.

It was a helluva night, and a kick to be on one of the biggest shows on t.v.. I couldn't stay for the after=show, though. I had to get to the airport and catch my flight back to Nashville. Blake thanked me, told me I did a great job and said he appreciated me coming on such short notice.

The flight was 3 ½ hours and I was back in my loft in Printer's Alley, above Bourbon Street Blues and Boogie Bar, by 4 a.m.. I fell right into bed and didn't wake up until 10 a.m. the next morning . . .

———

Having co-written a hit novelty song allowed me a certain

degree of autonomy in Nashville. I didn't need an agent or a manager when people like Blake Shelton or Gretchen Wilson would call me from time to time to play for them. The occasional royalty check from the song kept my bank account fairly healthy, which was why I wasn't concerned with how much I was going to be paid for *The Voice* appearance. I knew Blake would be fair.

I was having breakfast of cereal with grapes and milk when my cell phone rang. Seeing that it was Harley Rayborn, my mentor in the private eye business, I answered right away.

"Hey, Harley, how are you?" Harley had recently been diagnosed with colon cancer, and his treatments weren't going all that well.

"Saw you on the Voice last night, kid, with Shelton," Harley said. "You looked good!"

"Thanks, Harley," I said, "but how are you doing?"

"My ass hurts, kid, how d'ya think I'm doin'?" Harley said. "But I've got a case."

"Jesus, man, you're working? You can't even get around. Should you be—"

"No, no, I mean, I got a case for you," Harley said. "Can you pop around?"

"Yeah, sure," I said. "I'll come by in a little while, Harley."

"And bring hotdogs!"

"What about your nurse?"

"I'll send her on an errand. Let's synchronize our watches to make sure she's gone by the time you get here."

We agreed I'd stop by at 1, and hung up.

Zackie's in Germantown was out of the way, but that's where Harley liked to get his hotdogs, so I drove there first before going to his house in South Nashville.

I parked out front. Before going to the front door I circled around to the back and set the bag of hotdogs carefully on a window sill, hoping cats or dogs wouldn't get to it.

Then I went to the front door and knocked. It was opened by Harley's nurse, a middle-aged woman with stern features and a heart of gold. His doctor had recommended Miss Avery to him, and Harley was very happy with her. The same could not be said for her, though. He hardly ever did what she told him to do and I thought she deserved a medal for putting up with him.

"Mr. Velez," she said. "Come in. Harley told me you were coming."

"Good afternoon, Miss Avery," I said.

I stepped inside and she closed the door then turned to face me. In the beginning she wore a nurse's uniform, but after a few weeks she started wearing regular clothes, usually jeans and a colorful top. She was a husky woman who wasn't worried about looking lumpy in her clothes. The extra heft came in handy if she had to lift Harley into bed, out of a tub or—to his embarrassment—onto the toilet.

"Do I need to search you, Mr. Velez?"

I raised my hands in the air. "I swear I have no illicit food or drink on me."

"Cigars?"

"No."

She frowned at me.

"Go ahead and search, Miss Avery."

Instead she waved at me and said, "Go on in, then. He's still in bed, waiting for you. Let me know if he needs any more water."

"Yes, Ma'am."

I went down the hall to Harley's bedroom, knocked on the open door and went in.

"At last!" he said, from the bed. "Where are my dogs? Did Nurse Ratchet take them away from you? Don't tell me you let her take 'em—whataya doin'?"

I walked to the window, opened it, and brought the brown bag in from the window sill.

"Smart man!" he said, lowering his voice. "Gimme!"

I handed the dogs over to him. What did it matter? Only last week the doctors had sent Harley home "to die," as he put it. His cancer had spread and it was "only a matter of time."

As he unwrapped one and bit into it his eyes almost rolled back in his head.

"This is what I needed, kid."

"Any word?" I asked. "I mean, uh, any change in the, uh, prognosis?"

"Nope," he said, "still dyin'."

"You need something to drink?" I asked.

"I need a beer, but there's none in the house," he said, sourly, a dab of mustard in the corner of his mouth. "I got some water here."

He was eating the hotdog quickly, in case "Nurse Ratchet" came in. Harley figured he was dying anyway, he might as well eat what he wanted. He once told me if a doctor told him he could live 5 more years by never eating another hotdog, he'd say, "Take 'em. How good could the last five years of m life be if you can't eat a hot dog?"

I didn't used to agree with him, but lately I was having second thoughts.

"Oh, siddown, kid," Harley said. "You know, in that

chair so you can see down the hall and warn me if she's comin'."

"Right, right."

I sat down in the old chair, the same one I always sat in when I visited him. It actually did cut through the smell of death, because it smelled like it was a hundred years old— but I didn't mind.

He hurriedly took the second hotdog out and unwrapped it. He looked even thinner than the last time I'd seen him. His fingers looked longer, with yellowed nails and big, knobby knuckles.

As he bit into the second one I asked, "What's this about a case?"

"I got a call about a missing person," Harlan said. "Since I can't leave this damn house without fallin' on my face, I told them I'd pass the case along to you."

"To me?" I asked. "By name. Or did you say you'd pass it on to another investigator?"

"To you," he said. "I figured you'd take the case."

"Why is that?"

Harley pointed with the butt end of the second hot dog.

"I'm gonna let you find that out for yourself."

"Is this going to pay well?" I asked.

"That'll be up to you, kid," Harley said. "I don't negotiate your fees."

"Well," I said, "who will I be negotiating with?"

"I got that here someplace," Harley said, looking over at the night table next to the bed. "Here it is." He grabbed a piece of paper and held it out to me. I got up and took it from him, trying to avoid the mustard stain he left on it.

"That's the guy's name and phone number," Harley said. "I told him you'd call."

"When did you speak with him?"

"Yesterday." He popped the last piece of hotdog into his mouth. "He's waitin' for your call."

I looked at the name on the paper, and caught my breath.

"This says Carter Bannister."

"So?"

"Carter Bannister used to be one of the biggest agents in the business, Harley."

"What business?"

"The music business. The business I'm in."

"I didn't know that." He took the bottle of water from the night table and drank from it. "Used to be?"

"In the old days. I didn't even know he was still around."

"Well, he is," Harley said, "and he's waitin' to hear from you."

I took a napkin from the bag the hotdogs had come in, wiped the mustard off the paper, and then put it in my shirt pocket. I was wearing my Leon Russell pocket tee that day.

"I'll call him today."

"Good."

"You want to play some checkers, or something?" I asked.

"Naw," Harley said, "get the hell out of here. The place stinks like death. Go and call this feller and let me know what happens. Okay?"

"Okay, Harley. Thanks."

As he put his head back and closed his eyes, I walked down the hall to the front of the house. Miss Avery was sitting in the livingroom, reading a book.

"Here," she said, holding some envelopes out to me.

"More bills?" I asked.

She nodded. As the hospital bills came into the house,

she kept them from Harley and gave them to me when I visited. The old reprobate had no idea I was footing his bills. Both Miss Avery and I convinced him that the expenses—including her fees—were being covered by some insurance provided by social security. If Harley ever found out I was paying them, he'd tear me a new asshole

"Thank you, Miss Avery."

"Did he eat the hotdogs?" she asked, without looking up.

"What? Oh, uh, well, yeah."

She looked at me.

"Later, when he's puking them up, I'll remind him that you brought them to him."

"Look, Ma'am—"

"Never mind," she said, "he'll just say they were good going down. He won't hold it against you."

"No, he won't," I said, "but maybe I should hold it against myself."

"Maybe you should." She turned her attention back to her book.

I started for the door, opened it she spoke to me, again without looking.

"Bring him a beer, next time."

"What?" Did I hear her right?

"But just one."

CHAPTER 2

AFTER LEAVING Harley's I drove back home and gave
Elton Mott a call. Mott was like me, a musician for hire.
Last time I'd worked with him was a session for Keith
Urban. I thought of Elton when I was trying to come up
with somebody to call about Carter Bannister.

We caught up a bit on what we were each doing, and
then I asked him.

"Carter Bannister?" he said. "Is that old buzzard still
workin'?"

"That's what I was gonna ask you, dude," I said.

"I ain't heard nothin' about him in years," Elton said.
"Didn't even know if he was still alive."

"He ever work with a partner?"

"Not that I heard, bro," Elton said. "Jeez, he repped
some big names in his day."

"Yeah, he did," I said.

"Whataya think he wants with you, Auggie?"

It wasn't a crack, but an honest question.

"He doesn't want me, exactly," I said. "He was looking
for a detective and called Harley Rayborn."

"How is old Harley?"

"Not good," I said, but didn't go any further. "He referred the case to me—whatever the case is."

"He didn't give you any idea?"

"Said something about a missing person."

"Well," Elton said, "I'd give the old geezer a call, Auggie. He's a pipeline right back to the old days, and some big names. No tellin' where that might lead you. I heard he repped Glen Campell for a while, but I ain't sure."

"I'll ask him," I promised, "and let you know."

▭

After I hung up on Elton I took out Harley's note and dialed the number for Carter Bannister.

"Bannister Agency," a woman's voice answered.

"I'd like to speak with Mr. Bannister, please."

"Who's calling?"

"My name's Auggie Velez," I said.

"And what's it about? Are you seeking representation?"

"No," I said, "I was referred by Harley Rayborn."

"Just a minute."

She put me on hold, and then a man's voice came on.

"Mr. Velez?"

"That's right."

"Carter Bannister, here."

I hesitated. The man on the other end of the line sounded young. Not what I expected, at all.

"You're Carter Bannister?" I asked.

"The third," he said. "I can hear your confusion. You're thinking of my grandfather."

"Grandfather?"

"He was the one who started this agency, represented many of the early country superstars."

"Yes, he was," I said. "I didn't know the agency still existed."

"It didn't," the man said. "My grandfather retired, closed it up. I reopened it."

"What about your father?"

"He's not involved," Bannister said. "Can you come and see me, Mr. Velez? I have a job that needs doing."

"So I understand," I said. "A missing person, right?"

"Sort of," Bannister said. "I'll tell you about it when you get here."

"What's your address?"

He gave me the number of a building on Music Row, which figured.

"It's just down the street from where Noshville used to be."

"I know where it is," I said.

"I mention that," he said, "because I wonder if you'd mind bringing some bagels and coffee?"

CHAPTER 3

ALTHOUGH THE BUILDING had housed the offices of many record labels, and agencies connected to the business, when I got off the elevator at the 6th floor and entered the offices of the Bannister Agency, I was surprised at how stark and unassuming it was. The reception area was just a desk, and a girl seated behind it. The walls—where you usually would see photos, album covers, or gold records—were bare.

"Oh God," the girl at the reception desk said, "you brought food."

I raised the Einstein Bros. bag with the bagels in it. It would have been a Noshville bag if the place hadn't closed recently. "I didn't know what kind, so I brought a variety."

"And coffee?"

I had the carrier in the other hand with 6 large cups.

"Same thing. Didn't know how you folks took it."

She got up and came around the desk, a woman in a skirt and blouse, wearing flat shoes, very young and pretty.

"Let me have that stuff," she said. "You go in and see Carter and I'll bring this in."

"Okay, doll," I said. I handed her the bag and the carrier. "Which door?"

"That one," she said, jerking her pretty chin. "Which coffee is yours?"

"Black, no sugar."

"Okay. I'll bring it right in. Does the bagel matter?"

"Any kind'll do."

I went to the door she indicated, knocked and opened it.

"Mr. Velez," a man said effusively, rushing around from behind a desk. The office was much the same. Nothing on the walls, no excess furniture. Just a desk, a couple of chairs, and some file cabinets.

"Thanks for coming." He shook my hand with a lot of energy. In fact, his lean body vibrated with it. If he was 30 I'd be surprised. He had one of those smooth-skinned faces with cheeks always rosy, looking as if they'd never been touched by a razor.

"Have a seat," he said. "Did you, uh, bring the bagels?"

"And coffee," I said. "I left them with your girl."

"That's Nancy," he said, going back around his desk.

"She's a good kid."

"She said she'd bring 'em in."

His jacket was hanging on the back of his chair, and his shirt sleeves were rolled up. He had no tie, and his shirt was open at the collar. I sat and looked around.

"I know," he said, "it doesn't look like much right now. But it will. I'm gonna put the Bannister Agency back on the map."

Nancy came in with a tray and set it down on the desk. two cups of coffee and 4 bagels. I'd asked for butter and cream cheese on the side, and she'd brought them along with a couple of plastic knives. She was still chewing whichever bagel she'd taken for herself.

"Thanks for this," Bannister said. "I can have Nancy reimburse you out of petty cash."

The girl made a rude sound with her mouth on the way out. I looked at Bannister.

"She's right," he said, sheepishly, "I don't have enough in petty cash to pay for these bagels." He grabbed one.

"That sounds like you don't have the money to hire me, either," I said.

"You're right, I don't. Have a bagel."

I grabbed my coffee and drank from it while he smeared his bagel with cream cheese.

"Why am I here, Mr. Bannister?" I asked. "I mean, besides delivering the bagels and coffee?"

"Okay," Bannister said, "you brought the bagels, so you know I'm broke. I'm gonna level with you."

"That'd be nice."

"My grandfather retired a long time ago, but he kept up the rent on this place. When I told him I wanted to bring his agency back, he let me have it—but it's all I've got. The name, and this place."

"Where do I fit in?"

"I want you to find somebody for me."

"That's the word I got. Who is it?"

"You know the name Hammer Dylan?"

"Dylan?" I said, shocked. "Hammer Dylan? Jesus, I haven't heard that name—he disappeared . . . what? Forty years ago?"

"Forty-one," Bannister said. "He had the potential to be my grandfather's biggest client ever. The old man is still cashing checks on Dylan's name."

"And where's he sending Dylan's share?"

"He says he's keepin' it for him, for when he shows up again."

"And he thinks he will?"

"He's always thought that," Bannister said, smearing another bagel. "Always talking about when the Hammer comes back."

"How old would he be now?"

"Hammer'd be about . . . seventy-five, maybe more."

"He only ever made that one album, right?" I asked.

"That's right," Bannister said, "'Outlaw Dreams.'"

"That's right," I repeated, in awe. "'Outlaw Dreams' Man, what an album. That had some wicked guitar work on it."

"I want you to find him for me, Mr. Velez," Bannister said. "Hammer's the only way I'm gonna get this agency off the ground again."

"Are you sure your grandfather doesn't know where he is?" I asked.

He shrugged. "Maybe he does, but he won't tell me. You can ask him, if you want."

"What about his other clients?"

"I told you, he retired," Bannister said. "All his old clients are happy with the representation they now have. That is, the clients who are still alive."

I shook my head. "Hammer Dylan." I grabbed a sesame bagel, added some butter and took a bite. "Be one helluva an honor to meet him."

"Then you'll do it?"

"There's the question of my fee."

"I thought you said it'd be an honor."

"It would, but I still have bills to pay. How were you intending to pay me?"

"By giving you a piece of the action," Bannister said.

"I don't have any desire to be an agent, Mr. Bannister."

"Call me Carter," he said. "Look, once I've got Hammer

re-signed, I know some other artists will fall in line. It won't be too hard for me to raise ten grand for you—if you'll wait a while."

"Ten thousand, huh?"

"And the chance to meet Hammer."

"If he's even still alive."

"I'm pretty sure he is," Bannister said.

"And even if he is, what if he's not ready for a comeback?" I asked.

"That's a bridge I can cross when the time comes."

"Okay," I said, "let's say I'm in. His album is still available, right?"

"It came out on vinyl and has made all the moves since then—8-track, cassette, CD, MP3, and it's available now on iTunes for download. And, since vinyl's making a comeback. There, too."

"Still with the same label?"

Bannister nodded and said, "Starcade Records."

"Oh, shit," I said.

"What's the matter."

"That's Corky Barnes' outfit."

"You know Barnes?"

"I do."

"Well, that's good."

I lifted the bagel to my mouth again and before taking a bite to get the bad taste out of my mouth said, "If you knew Corky Barnes you wouldn't say that."

CHAPTER 4

CORKY BARNES WAS NOT my favorite person, so I wasn't in a hurry to talk to him. I put that dubious pleasure off for a while.

I had some more questions for Carter Bannister III, mostly about his grandfather.

"What about your other clients? Would any of them know anything about Hammer? I mean, are any of them his contemporaries?"

"The only contemporaries I know of," Bannister said, "would be like Willie Nelson and Kris Kristofferson."

"Do you think they'd talk to me?"

"I don't know," he said, with a shrug. "I don't know them personally. And as far as other clients . . . don't have any. Hammer's going to be my first."

"If I find him."

"Right."

"Would your grandfather talk to me?" I asked.

"I think so," he said. "I'll call him. You'd probably have to go to his house, though. He doesn't leave there very often. He's eighty-three."

"Where does he live?"

"Brentwood."

I whistled.

"I'm gonna need a passport to get in there," I said.

He laughed. "Like I said, maybe just a phone call."

"When can you do that?"

"Well . . . now?"

"Now's good," I said. "Might as well get this show on the road."

"So you'll take the case?"

"I'll take the case now," I said, reminding him, "for ten grand later."

"That's the deal."

"Then make the call."

He took out his cell phone.

—

20 minutes later I was in my car heading for Brentwood. Neither of my businesses had yet taken me out there to the multi-million dollars homes of some of Nashville's biggest stars and business people. When I'd mentioned needing a passport I was only half kidding. To most normal people, Brentwood is like another country.

I was no longer nursing the 2002 Toyota I'd been driving for years. I'd switched to a 2012 Toyota Camry. I don't spend my money on new cars because they mean so little to me. I just use them to get me from here to there.

When I drove up to the front gates they were open, which was a surprise. I decided to be polite and ring the bell, anyway.

"Yes?" a woman asked.

"Hello, my name's Auggie Velez. I'm here to see Mr. Bannister. I believe I'm expected?"

"Well, yes," she said, impatiently, "that's why the gate is open. Drive up to the house."

I was going to say "thank you" but heard the intercom click off, so I just got back in my car and drove up to the front door, which opened as I got there.

I assumed the handsome, middle-aged woman standing in the doorway was the impatient one I'd spoken to on the intercom as I once again got out of my car and approached the door.

"Mr. Velez?" She was giving my Leon Russell tee shirt a disapproving look.

I wanted to give her back some of her attitude and ask "Who else did you think it'd be after we just spoke?" but instead I said, "That's right."

"He's waiting for you by the pool. Please, follow me."

She turned and went into the house, leaving me to pull the front door closed behind us. We walked across a lot of marble tile to get to the pool behind the house. I got an impression of very stark furnishings along the way, and then we were outside and walking down 3 steps to more tile.

An old man in a loud Hawaiian shirt, bright yellow shorts and a large brimmed straw hat reclined on a lounge chair near the edge of the pool. On the table next to him was a pitcher of something that looked like iced tea. There were two glasses. His will full, and I assumed the empty one was for me.

"Are you Velez?" he asked. He was so thin I was shocked at how big and booming his voice was.

"I am."

"I'm Carter Bannister, the Original," he said. "Have a seat. Iced tea?"

"Sure."

"Vangie, can you pour?"

As I sat in the chair across the table from him the woman stepped forward and filled my glass.

"Anything else, Papa?" she demanded.

"No, dear," he said. "You can go and do whatever it is you have to do."

"Run your house," she grumbled, "that's what I do. Pay your bills, do your laundry, clean your . . ." it faded out as she went back up the steps and into the house.

"Your daughter?"

"Daughter-in-law," he said, "Evangeline. It was her son you talked to this mornin'. The third. Her husband, my late son, was the second. His mother's stupid idea. I think men should have their own names."

"She doesn't seem to be very, uh, happy."

"That's just because I'm still alive."

CHAPTER 5

"EXCUSE ME?"

"She's waitin' for me to die so everythin' I have will be hers," he explained. He leaned forward and lowered his voice. "She thinks I have a ton of money."

"And you don't?" I asked.

"I have money," he said, sitting back, "but a lot less than she thinks. And it ain't gonna go to her, no matter how much laundry she does."

"But if she pays your bills—"

"I give her access to just enough," he said, with a smile that revealed yellowed teeth. I'd seen those teeth on many long-time smokers in the past.

"Okay—" he started, then abruptly started to cough. It went on a while, coming from deep in his chest, and then he took a few sips of iced tea before it subsided. I wondered if it was just a product of all that smoking, or if it was full-blown cancer. He didn't look nearly as far gone as Harley, but that didn't mean he wasn't afflicted.

"Okay," he said, leaning back again to relax, "so my grandson says you've agreed to help him find ol' Hammer."

"I have," I said, "for a price."

"Of course," Bannister said. "There's always a price. That only makes sense. Only a fool works for free."

"I couldn't agree more."

"That's my grandson, the fool," he said. "Right now he's workin' for nothin'."

"I guess he thinks that'll change if I can find Hammer."

"Hammer's dead," Bannister said.

"You're sure about that?"

He leaned forward. "If he was alive, I'd've heard from him by now."

"What about his royalty checks?" I asked.

"What about them?"

"Your grandson said you've been sending Hammer his royalty checks."

"That ain't exactly right," Bannister said. "I been sendin' them somewhere. And somebody's been cashin' them."

"But you don't think it's Hammer."

"I don't."

"Why not?"

"It ain't his signature on the backs of the checks."

"You can tell that?"

"I knew Hammer longer and better than anybody," Bannister said. "I saw him sign contracts and checks. Yeah, I can tell."

"So what if he's got somebody signing for him?" I asked.

"Well, that'll be for you to find out."

"Did Hammer have any family?"

"Nope," Bannister said, "he was an orphan. I was his only family."

"No wife?"

"Lots of women," Bannister said. "No wife, and no girl-friend. Just lots of women."

"How did he get along with other artists?"

"He didn't," Bannister said. "He had an attitude, and they all hated him. Willie, Waylon, Johnny, Hank, . . . nobody liked him."

"Where did you get this address that you're sending the checks to?"

"Hammer gave it to me forty years ago. When he signed with me I asked him how he wanted to be paid, and he said to send the checks there."

"Will you give me the address?" I asked.

"It's a post office box, but yeah, Vangie's got it. She'll give it to you."

"She will?" My tone betrayed what I was thinking.

"Don't worry," he said, "she won't hurt you. She'll give it to you."

"Well," I said, "then I guess that's it. Thanks for talking to me."

"I'm just tryin' to help the kid," he said. "He wants to get the agency goin' again, more power to 'im."

"How's his mother feel about it?"

"Maybe you better ask her."

"How do I find her?" I asked. "It's a big house."

"It's real big," he said, "twenty-four rooms, but we only use about six of 'em. Don't worry, when you go in, she'll hear you and she'll find you."

———

I went back into the house, over the marble tiles again, and sure enough, before I could retrace my steps to the front door Bannister's daughter-in-law, Vangie, appeared.

"Are you finished?" she asked. She looked as if she had just expertly applied a new layer of make-up. It made her look younger, and prettier.

"Not quite," I said. "Your father-in-law said you'd give me the address he's been sending Hammer Dylan's royalty checks to."

Her face assumed a put upon expression and she said, "Follow me."

We went through a dining room that had a long wooden table and 4 chairs around it, but no other furniture. I followed her into a large room with a deep piled, pale carpet, what looked like an antique sofa and matching chair, and a small French writing desk. I assumed this was where she sat when she paid all his bills.

She sat in a matching chair, opened a drawer, took out a slip of paper, wrote down an address and handed the paper to me. It was a post office box in a Tennessee town I never heard of, called Anthem.

"You have the address memorized?"

"I've sent a lot of checks there over the years," she said. "Anything else?"

"Do you know anything about this town? Anthem?"

"Never heard of it."

"Could it be where Hammer was born?"

"Who knows? That's for you to find out, isn't it?"

"Yes," I said, "it is. How do you feel about your son's attempt to reopen your father-in-law's agency?"

"It doesn't matter how I feel," she said. "It's never mattered to the men in my life how I felt about anything, so I don't have an opinion."

"What about your son's father?"

"He died about ten years ago," she said. "Now there's only my father-in-law, my son, and me."

"Do you know anything your father-in-law doesn't know?"

She frowned at me. "How do you mean?"

"Anything that might help me find Hammer Dylan."

She looked disgusted. "Dylan's dead."

"Are you sure?"

"If he's not dead he's eighty," she said. "What good is he gonna do anyone?"

"Willie Nelson seems to be doing okay."

All she said to that was, "Hmph."

"Well, is it all right if I leave you my card?" I asked. "If you think of anything helpful you can give me a call."

"Whatever," she said. "My father-in-law told me I had to cooperate."

I took out my card and handed it to her.

"This says you're a musician."

I never bothered to have two cards made up. I only used the 1, and mostly I needed people to be able to get ahold of me for gigs.

"I do both," I said.

"Guitar?"

"Yes," I said, "and I'm a song writer."

Most people come back with "Anything I might have heard?" but she just put the card down on her desk and ignored it.

"Thanks for your help," I said.

"I'll walk you out."

She led me to the front door, then stood in the doorway, watched me get into my car and drive away. I guess she wanted to make sure I was gone.

CHAPTER 6

I WENT BACK to my place above the Bourbon Street Blues and Boogie Bar in Printer's Alley, and put *Outlaw Dreams* on my stereo. I owned the album in both Vinyl and CD, and chose the vinyl because it was the original.

I sat at my desk across from the guitars I had on stands and read the liner notes on the album. It was a lot of double-talk, not really giving any real information about Hammer, with lots of photos of him in a black hat, denim shirt and jeans, holding a guitar, playing it, walking with it over his shoulder, usually with a cigarette hanging from his mouth. You couldn't have used any of them to pick him out on the street. The photos all seemed shot to intentionally hide his face.

So there were things I'd never noticed about the cover and liner notes before, but the music, that was still the same —soulful in some places, soulless in others, but mostly brilliant, even from an artist so young and new.

He had come along 11 years after Bob Dylan, and I wondered now—I hadn't back then—about the last name, and if it was deliberate? Maybe he wanted his albums displayed right next to Dylan's? Or maybe that really was his last name. In point of fact, it wasn't even Bob Dylan's real name, he had been born Robert Allen Zimmerman.

I listened to the entire album, then slipped it back into the sleeve and put it away. I had a small collection of vinyl, just albums I wanted to keep in their original form—a few Leon Russell, Johnny Cash (including The *Highwaymen* CD, with Waylon, Willie and Kristofferson), Bobbie Gentry's *Fancy* (just a personal favorite), Bonnie Raitt's *Nick of Time*, Tanya Tucker's *Delta Dawn* (don't ask) and some others.

After that I wrote the checks to pay the bills Harley's nurse had given me. Luckily, the checks for my novelty song "Stan, Stan the Pool Man (or Drowning in Your Love) were continuing to come in at a record pace. It had been used in 3 commercials, and 1 movie over the past year. That gave me enough money to be self-sufficient, work on both my careers when I wanted to, and pay Harley's medical bills.

Realizing I was hungry I walked to 4th and Broadway and went into the Back Alley Diner on Arcade. It was only about a block away as the crow flies, but if I stuck to the streets it was longer. So I cut through the post office parking lot (pausing to mail the bills), since the P.O. was right next to it. It had only been around about a year, but the family had been in the restaurant business for over 30.

I ate with my cell phone sitting on the table next to my elbow. It was a bad habit I'd picked up—like most cell phone users—but I never knew when I was going to get a call about a gig, or from Harley about, well, something else that I dreaded.

I'd been waiting months for Harley to die. It sounded cruel, but was true. He'd already lasted half a year longer than the doctors had said. The call could come any day. It was one I dreaded, but was inevitable, so you can see why I'd want to get it over with.

I was finishing my burger when the cell phone buzzed. I checked the screen and it took me a moment to realize whose number it was.

"Bannister?" I said.

"It's Nancy," his girl said.

"What's up?"

"Mr. Bannister wanted me to call and check on your progress."

"After half a day?"

"You went and spoke with his grandfather, right?"

"Yes."

"How did that go?"

"Fine, I guess," I said. "I got what I could from him, and from his daughter-in-law."

"His daughter-in-law?"

"Yes," I said, "your boss' mother."

"Geez," she said, "he hasn't spoken to her in years."

"Huh, I didn't get that from her," I said, "but then I didn't get much."

"So you didn't find Hammer?"

"Not yet, Nancy," I said. "Tell your boss it's gonna take me a little bit longer than this."

"All right," she said, "I'll tell him."

"And don't call me again," I said. "I'll give him a call when I have something."

"Okay, fine," she said, and hung up. It sounded like I pissed her off, but that was okay. I didn't want them calling me every day for updates. I didn't work that way.

I put my cell phone down, had the last bite of my burger, my last fry and my last onion ring. It was something I recently noticed I did, eating my food in equal increments, so that I finished everything at about the same time. I washed it all down with the last of my Coke, and signaled to the waitress for my check.

I paid the bill, pocketed by cell, and left.

———

I walked one block to 4th and Commerce, then turned right to walk Printer's Alley when my phone buzzed. I almost let it go, thinking it was Nancy again. But when I took it out and looked, I saw that it wasn't.

"Hey, Elton."

"What are you doin' right now, dude?" Elton asked.

"Just walkin' down Commerce on my way home," I said. "'sup?"

"I've got somebody you might want to talk to."

"About what?"

"About Carter Bannister," Elton said. "I was doin' some research, and came across somethin'."

"Somethin' good?"

"I dunno," Elton said, "but it's gonna cost you to find out."

"How much?"

"Beer," he said, "it's gonna cost you some beer."

CHAPTER 7

ELTON WAS EASY TO FIND. He was playing that night at the club I lived above, the Bourbon Street Blues and Boogie Bar.

I'd played the Boogie Bar on occasion myself, but tonight I was just having a drink with my buddy.

"You on tonight?" the bartender asked, as I took a stool between two other guys, both of whom were hitting on girls. It was early and the club wasn't in full swing yet, so a stool was easy to find. Still, it was noisy. Men were already busy trying to pick up girls, and the girls were already busy trying to decide which man they'd allow to pick them up.

I looked at the bartender, thought I recalled his name was Craig.

"No, Craig," I said. "I'm just meeting Elton."

"He was doin' a sound check," the bartender said. "Should be around." He didn't correct me, so I must have been right about his name.

"I'll take a beer and wait," I said. "Yazoo."

The Boogie Bar had lots of beers on tap and in bottles, from Bud and Miller to Fat Tire and Stella, but they had the local Yazoo Pale Ale on tap, and I preferred it to the others. Occasionally, though, I'd sample one of their selections of Louisiana beers: Abita, or Blackened Voodoo. Not tonight, though.

"Craig set my beer down and asked, "What's with the hat?"

I had taken to wearing a baseball cap that said MUSIC CITY on the front.

"I was hanging out with a girl who told me bandanas were passé," I told him. "She gave me this."

"What happened?"

"I kept the hat," I said, "but not the girl."

He laughed and went off to serve two more customers.

I was taking my first sip when Elton came up behind me and slapped me on the back. I avoided choking, or spilling, and turned to look at him.

Elton Mott was my age, early 30's, but I hadn't seen him in a while and since then he'd grown some chin whiskers. I didn't have the heart to tell him he looked like Shaggy from Scooby Doo.

"How ya doin', Auggie?" He spoke loudly, to be heard above the din, and the music hadn't even started yet. I had the feeling I was getting old fast, because I didn't like being in noisy clubs, anymore.

"Heya, dude," I said. "Beer?"

"Does a shit bear in the woods?" he asked, cackling. Obviously, he'd already had a few. Elton usually got a little tanked before going on stage.

I waved down the bartender and got two more beers. The man on my left must have said something right, because he and the girl got up and left. Elton took his stool and bumped me with his shoulder.

"What happened with Bannister?"

"It wasn't the old man," I told him, "it was the grandson. He's trying to restart the agency."

"And he wants you?"

"As a detective, not an artist," I said, "and I told you, he wanted Harley. He ended up with me."

"And how did he feel about that?"

"He's probably better off," I said. "He has no money and Harley wouldn't have worked for free."

"But you will?"

"He succeeded in attracting my interest."

"How'd he do that?"

"By mentioning Hammer Dylan."

"Dylan!" Elton said, shaking his head. "Why's he interested in a dead old timer." He was puzzled.

"Because he doesn't believe he's dead," I said, "and he'd like me to find him."

"Wow," Elton said. "You bought that?"

"Like I said, I'm interested. I went and talked to the old man."

"What did he have to say?"

"That Hammer's dead," I answered. "He said he'd know if he was alive."

"How?"

"Says Hammer would've been in touch with him, by now."

"You believe 'im?"

"I believe he believes it."

"And the kid?"

"I think he's hopin'."

"So why go along with him, and not the grandfather?"

"Because if Hammer Dylan is alive," I said. "I'd like to be the one who finds him. I'd like to talk to him."

"And maybe jam with him?"

I grinned. "Wouldn't that be somethin'?"

"Yeah, it would," Elton said, "but he's dead. He's jammin' with Elvis and Johnny Cash."

"Now that would really be somethin'," I said. "Look, before you have to go on, what did you want to tell me that I might find interestin'? Somethin' about the kid, Bannister?"

"No, not the kid," Elton said, "the old man."

"What do you know about him?"

"Nothin'," Elton said, "only what I told you. But I found a guy who might know somethin'."

"Who?"

"His name's Hoyt Bennett. He used to be called 'Axe Man' Bennett."

"Axe Man Bennett?" I repeated in surprise. "I've heard of him. He was a helluva guitar player in the old days. Hey, wait a minute . . . did he play with Hammer Dylan?"

"On his one album," Elton said, nodding "Only he says there was more than one."

"More than one Hammer Dylan album?"

Elton shrugged. "According to Bennett. I spoke to him about Bannister, but he was the one who brought up Dylan. And that was before I knew you were lookin' for him."

"Where does he live?"

"I don't know."

"Well, where did you find him?"

"I didn't," Elton said. "He found me. I told you, I was doin' some research for you."

"Where?"

"Axe Man."

"What?"

"The Axe Man," Elton said. "It's a music store."

"I thought I knew every place in Nashville that sold guitars."

"They sell more than guitars," Elton said. "Sheet music, other instruments, even some paperbacks."

"Where is it?"

"At the very end of Music Row," Elton said. "Been there for years. So has Bennett."

"He works there?"

"He owns it," Elton said. "He sits there all day, behind the register, and tells stories."

"To who?"

"Anybody who'll listen."

"And he'll tell me about Hammer Dylan?"

"He said he can tell you . . . things. He wasn't specific, but I thought he'd be worth talkin' to."

"All right," I said, "I'll talk to him. I'll go by tomorrow. Think he'll be there?"

"He's there every day."

"Why don't I know about this store?" I asked.

"You really wanna know?"

"Yeah."

"You're a snob, Auggie," he said. "When it comes to your guitars, you're a snob."

"Fuck you, Elton."

He laughed, got off his stool and slapped me on the shoulder.

"Stay for some music?"

"I'm tired," I said. "Maybe next time."

"Thanks for the beer."

"Thanks for the help."

"Thank me if Axe Man actually does help," he said.

CHAPTER 8

I WENT to Music Row the next morning. The Axe Man Music store stood back from the street and down a few steps. This explained why, with all the time I had spent on Music Row, I had never seen it before. It was pretty much dwarfed and buried by all the larger buildings around it.

The front window was so dusty I could hardly see through it. Displayed there were some old instruments—a trumpet, a saxophone, a violin—yellowed sheet music and paperbacks. The front door was old, blistered wood, once painted green, now faded.

I went inside. The door squeaked loudly, so it didn't need an entry bell ballyhooing my arrival.

The inside was musty, smelled of dust and old books. It didn't look or feel like a place I'd ever buy a guitar from, but there they were, on the walls, all makes and models.

Even more mystified that I had never heard of a place with a selection of guitars like this, I approached a slightly raised desk where I assumed business was done. When I got there and old timer behind it glanced at me. His head was down, but his eyes peered up over his glasses.

"Yeah?"

"Are you Hoyt Bennett, the Axe Man?"

Now he took off the glasses and looked directly at me.

"Who wants to know?"

"My name's Auggie Velez," I said. "Elton Mott sent me over to talk to you."

His lined, lived-in, leathery face broke into a smile.

"Hell, why didn't you say so in the first place?" He extended his hand. I saw the callouses on his fingertips. "Happy to meet you."

"You, too," I said, shaking his hand. "Why haven't I ever seen this store before?"

"You have to know it's here," Bennett said, "or be lookin' for it, like you were today. You want some coffee? I got a pot in the back."

"What about your business?" I asked.

"Ah," he said, "I'll put the closed sign out. Like you said, who can find this place?"

He came around the desk, turned the OPEN sign to CLOSED, and then waved at me.

"Come on, we can talk in the back."

As we walked past the display wall of guitars I could see he had every make and model possible: Gibson, Fender, Yamaha, Epiphone, Sqier. He had everything from beginners to special editions. I spotted a Taylor 224ce-k Deluxe Grand that I knew went for $1500 easy. It had to take a whole lot of money to carry them all.

As we went through a curtained doorway into the back room he said, "You're wonderin' how I can afford to carry all those axes."

He grabbed a pretty full Mr. Coffee and filled two cups.

"Cream? Sugar?"

"Just like that, thanks,"

"Same here."

He handed me a white mug, kept the black one for himself. Then he stared at my shirt.

"Hey, cool, Leon," he said. "You wear a lot of those?"

"Different one every day."

"Wow, you must have a helluva collection."

I looked at the faded Jimi Hendrix he was wearing.

"I don't have that one."

"This?" He looked down. "Nobody does, man. I got this from Jimi when it first came out."

I felt my eyes go wide.

"You knew Jimi Hendrix?"

He smiled at me and said, with such pleasure, "I played with him, man."

I looked at him again. When I walked in I took him for 60 or so, but had had to be older than that to have played with Jimi.

"I can read your mind, man," he said. "I'm seventy-eight."

"You played with Jimi?"

"Not when he hit it big," Bennett said. "Him and me, we backed The Isley Brothers and Little Richard on the chitlin' circuit, then Jimi went off on his own."

"And what'd you do?"

"Knocked around for a while, played with the Allmans, but I was a little older than them fellas, and I didn't have the time or the real talent, so I hadda do other things."

"Like what?"

"I was a salesman for a while," he said. "Sold everythin' from vacuum cleaners to drugs. Taught for a while. But then I opened this place about thirty years ago, and I been here ever since."

"You must've been here when nothing else was."

"Oh yeah," he said, "all these building sprang up around me until I was buried alive." He said it with humor, not a note of rancor.

"Jesus, you must've seen a lot," I said. I remembered that Elton said Bennett sat behind his register and told stories. I wished I had time to listen to about a dozen of them. "Hey, did you ever play with Clapton?"

"Not on stage," he said, "but I jammed with him when he was between Cream and Derek and the Dominoes."

"Jesus!" I said. I don't know why, but I was buying everything he said. He could have told me at that moment that he gave Clapton the name Layla to write about, and I would have believed him. He didn't, though. (Layla was from 7th-century Arabia and later formed the basis of *The Story of Layla and Majnun* by the 12th-century Persian poet Nizami Ganjavi. It was a story of unrequited love that was related to Clapton while he was going through his own bout of the same for Pattie Boyd, the wife of George Harrison.)

I sipped the coffee. It was bad, but I didn't care.

"So, what's on your mind?" Bennett asked. "Elton said something about you and old Carter Bannister."

"Not the old man," I said, "the kid, who's taking over the business. He hired me to find Hammer Dylan."

"Hammer Dylan?" He seemed shocked.

"That's right."

"Hammer's dead."

"His grandson isn't so sure about that."

"Grandson?"

I nodded.

"Carter Bannister, the third," I said. "He's hoping to restart the agency."

"And he thinks ol' Hammer is still alive?"

I nodded.

"And where would he think Hammer's been all this time?" Bennett asked. "Hangin' out with Elvis? And before you ask, I never played with Elvis."

The question had been on the tip of my tongue. I was going to have to stop fanboying out and stick to business. But damn it, there was a Taylor 224 in the other room!

CHAPTER 9

"SO WHY'D young Bannister go to you?"

"It's something I do when I'm not gigging," I said. "I'm a private investigator."

"Well, cool!" he said. "A gui-tar playin' private eye!"

"Yeah," I said, "sometimes it's cool. Like now."

I studied Bennett a little more and realized he was from mixed parents. One must have been white, while the other was either black or Mexican, or something else exotic.

"Well, whataya want me to tell ya?" he asked.

"Whether or not Hammer's alive," I said. "I'm getting the feeling you know everybody in this business."

"As far as I know, Hammer's dead," he said, without hesitation.

"Okay," I said, "if he was alive, where would he be?"

"Mississippi."

"You say that with such conviction. Why Mississippi?"

"Hammer always felt such a connection with Robert Johnson," Bennett said. "So if he's anywhere he's at the Crossroads."

"And where would that Crossroads be?" I asked. "Has anyone ever said?"

"Clarksdale, Mississippi."

"Oh, yeah, I remember," I said, as it flashed on me. "Highway sixty one, wasn't it?"

"That's right," Bennett said, "the intersection of Old Highway sixty-one and Old Highway forty-nine. There even a sort of monument there, with three crossed swords."

"So you think Hammer's in Clarksdale."

"No," Bennett said, "you asked me where he'd be if he was alive."

"Oh, right. Okay, anywhere else I might look?"

"Well, Johnson did contact his first talent scout in Jackson, Mississippi. On the other hand, the first place he ever recorded was San Antonio, Texas. So . . ."

"So Hammer could be in San Antonio?"

"No," Bennett said, "I'd say Mississippi. That's where the legend says Johnson sold his soul to the devil."

"So Clarksdale or Jackson, Mississippi," I repeated.

"Clarksdale's a mud puddle," Bennett said. "I'd definitely say Jackson. If he was alive he'd be in hidin', right? So he'd want to be close to the spirit of Robert Johnson."

"How well did you know Hammer, Bennett?"

"My name's Hoyt," the man said, "Just call me Hoyt."

"Okay, Hoyt. How well did you know him?"

"As well as anybody, I guess. I played with him."

"Was he ever here?"

"You mean, right here? Yeah, he was here a time or two."

That was the first time I felt he wasn't being completely truthful.

"Okay, so did you ever hear him mention Jackson, Mississippi?"

Bennett stroked his long, stubble covered jaw.

"Yeah, I think he did talk about it a time or two. I mean, he talked about Robert Johnson a lot. Hammer once said he wondered if Johnson was out there doing the devil's work, buyin' souls of folks who wanted to play the guitar." He shook his head and chuckled.

"Okay," I said "I guess Jackson's a place to start. What can you tell me about the talent scout Robert Johnson contacted?"

"That'd be H.C. Speir," he said. "He was a big whig in that town, owned a record store down there, introduced Johnson to Don Law, who took him to San Antonio to record. But Speir and Law are both long dead.

Anybody connected to Robert Johnson must have been long dead. And the same could be said for Hammer Dylan —except maybe for Hoyt Bennett, the Axe Man, who seemed to be pointing me toward Jackson, Mississippi.

CHAPTER 10

BENNETT WALKED me to the front of the store.

"Where is Johnson buried?" I asked, as we walked.

"There are three gravesites," Bennett said. "All in Mississippi. You'd have to do the research. But there are claims at all three that they're the one true grave of Johnson. On the other hand . . ."

"Yes?"

"He died such a pauper that it's also possible he ended up in a potter's field, somewhere."

"That's right," I commented, "all his success and recognition came after he died."

"You know," he said, "when I heard Elton was asking about Hammer Dylan I thought somebody was lookin' for the second album."

"Oh yeah, he mentioned that," I said. "Tell me about that. You played on it?"

"Pretty much the last thing I ever did."

"Do you know where it is?"

"Not a clue," he said. "I think when Hammer disappeared—or died—it died with him."

"Or disappeared with him."

"Who knows?" Bennett said. "If he's alive, maybe he's still fine tuning that album. He sure was picky about what went on it."

As we walked past his display wall I looked up again at the collection.

"You wanna take one down, take it for a spin?" he asked. "The two-twenty five, maybe?"

"No, thanks," I said. "I think I'd be too . . . intimidated."

"No reason for that," he said. "You're good."

"What?"

"Oh yeah, I've heard you play. At the Ryman, and once at the Bluebird. You've got everything I never had, Auggie . . . talent. Elton told me he thinks you're the best guitar man in Nashville. Of course, he also asked me not to tell you he said so."

"That's a high compliment coming from him. I won't tell him you spilled the beans."

"Elton is good," he said, "technically. All the good ones have the technical skills, but the great ones . . ." He touched his chest. ". . . they had it here. That's where you have it, son."

"Thanks, Hoyt," I said. "Now that's high praise coming from you."

When they got to the front door Bennett turned his sign around to OPEN again before letting me out.

"Hoyt, one more question."

"What's that?"

"If Hammer is alive today, how old would he be?"

"Well, like most of those guys he was younger than me, so I guess he'd be about seventy-two or three"

"Thanks for your time, Hoyt."

"Come back real soon and we'll jam, son," he said. "I like to hear somebody good noodle with my stock."

"I'll be back," I promised. "You can be sure of it."

CHAPTER 11

NORMALLY I WOULD HAVE STOPPED in at the Noshville Deli on 19th and Broadway, but it had closed down when a developer bought the property, and all the space around it. So instead, I took a Broadway bus to Arcade Alley, near 4th, and went to the Back Alley Diner. It was between lunch and dinner, so I got a booth with no trouble, right at the window.

"What can I getcha?" the waiter asked.

"Coffee, for now. I may be joined by somebody else, so I'll wait to order."

"Sure thing."

I took out my cell and keyed in Carter Bannister the Third's number.

"Auggie," he said, excited to hear from me. "Do you have something already?"

"I might. How'd you like to meet me for an early dinner at the Back Alley Diner?"

"Um, I don't really have time—"

"On me."

"I'll be right there."

━━

15 minutes later Carter was sitting across from me with a cup of coffee. We had each put in our orders.

"Tell me about the second album, Carter," I said.

"What?"

"Hammer's second album," I said. "What do you know about it?"

He sat forward, his forearms on the table.

"What do *you* know about it?"

"I have a source who says he played on both Hammer's albums."

"So there is a second!" Carter said, excitedly. "I heard about it, but thought it was a myth."

"So is it Hammer you want?" I asked. "Or the second album?"

"Both, if I can get 'em. Maybe I can even get him to go on tour, and do a third album."

"On tour?" I asked. "Carter. He'd be in his early seventies if he's alive."

"Hey," Carter said, "Willie Nelson is still touring."

From what I'd heard of late, Willie's cancelling more dates than he's making, because of his health.

"So you knew about the second album all along and didn't tell me?" I asked.

"It's a myth," he explained. "I didn't think it was germane to what I wanted you to do."

"Find Hammer."

"Exactly."

"And if we happen to come up with the second album . . ."

" . . . so much the better."

The waiter came with our plates. We both went simple:

burger and fries. Carter attacked his like he hadn't eaten in weeks.

"Carter, can you talk to your grandfather again for me?" I asked. "See if he might have some idea where Hammer would be if he was still alive."

"What have you got so far?" he asked.

"A musician who played with Hammer thinks he'd be in Clarksdale, or Jackson, Mississippi."

"The Crossroads?"

"You've done your homework."

"My research, yeah," Carter said. "Why there?"

"Because he owed so much to Robert Johnson, apparently."

"Most musicians do owe a lot to Johnson," Carter said, "especially guitar players. Well, look who I'm talking to."

"Sorry," I said, "I owe more to Jimi and Clapton."

"Nevertheless," Carter said, "maybe you should take a ride down to Mississippi."

"I don't think so."

"Why not?"

"The musician who told me about the Crossroads," I said, "he seemed way too anxious for me to go to Mississippi."

"So you think Hammer's in Nashville?"

"I don't know where he is," I said, "I'm just saying I think I know where he isn't."

CHAPTER 12

WE SPLIT up in front of the Back Alley. Carter went back to his office, and I started walking. If I believed that Hammer Dylan was alive, and not in Mississippi, where did that leave me? Would he stay in Nashville, where he was likely to be recognized? Even if he wanted to stick close to home, wouldn't he have picked, say, Memphis? Or Knoxville?

Probably the best people in town to talk to would be the old timers, some of the older musicians in town who might have known Hammer. And I knew a few.

———

Talking to musicians in the evenings in Nashville meant club hopping. I hit Tin Roof, the Mercy Lounge, Legends Corner, The Stage on Broadway, BB King's Blues Bar, the Station Inn and Robert's Western World. My last stop of the night was The Bourbon Street Blues and Boogie Bar, so I'd be near home—literally, downstairs from my apartment.

I knew I'd have a drink every place I went and end of

buzzed, so I took cabs all night. That would certainly figure into my bill to Carter Bannister.

I spoke with Jess "the Mouth Organ" Willis, Bam-Bam McAllister, G-String Sammy Taylor and Bobby "the Bass" Stiletto. They were all in their 60's, just old enough to have possibly seen or played with Hammer Dylan in the early 70's.

Mouth Organ—who played a hot harmonica—said he had seen Hammer a few times in person, but never got to talk to him.

Bam-Bam McAllister said he had actually played drums in a session with Dylan, but they had never exchanged words outside the studio.

G-String Sammy—a pretty good guitar man—said he had dropped out of college to travel around and play gigs, and by the time he got back to Nashville, Hammer had come and gone.

And Bobby the Bass—not a gangster, despite the last name—said he jammed with some of Hammer's boys, but never with Hammer, himself.

"But they talked about him," Bobby added. "They said he had an ego the size of Texas, and often talked about going to his own funeral, because he wanted to see how many people would be there, mourning him."

That was the most I got out of anyone that night about Hammer Dylan.

And then I met Nikki.

———

For weeks the Bourbon had been bally-hooing the appearance on their stage of Nikki Rialto. She was a blues/country/rock chanteuse who had hit it big later in life than most artists, charting her first number one hit at 45 years old. Now in her 50's, she'd had a few hits on iTunes, toured the country opening for some of the biggest acts, but on occasion liked to come back home to Nashville and play the clubs.

This happened to be the night Nikki was appearing at the Bourbon, and the place was packed.

"Yazoo," I said to the bartender, grabbing an empty stool. It was Craig, again.

"Comin' up."

He came back with a frosty mug.

"You here for Nikki?" he asked.

"Actually, I forgot she was here tonight. I'm looking to talk to some old timers."

"Well, her guys are pretty young," he said.

"That may be," I said, "but she's not, right?"

"Hey," he said, leaning on the bar, "she might not be a spring chicken, but I gotta say, she's pretty hot."

I remembered Nikki's album covers. On the cover she was wearing a tank top, showing off her toned arms and nice shoulders. She had a lot of hair and a Bonnie Raitt vibe to her. But I had never seen her in person, so I was unprepared.

When she came on stage to raucous applause with 3 guys in their 20's and 30's, I saw what the bartender was talking about.

She was hot.

—

I watched her do her set, sitting there on a stool with a guitar. She was wearing a purple tank top and jeans. I watched the muscles in her arms move as she played and, as the set progressed she started to nip out, illustrating the fact that she had nothing on under the shirt. Finally—because no matter how well air-conditioned a club is, there's heat on stage—she started to sweat through the shirt. It was almost like being at a wet tee-shirt contest.

Nikki didn't have a pretty face, exactly, but she was sexy as hell. And she was one of those women who seemed to get better with age.

But I really didn't know what I was talking about, because I hadn't seen her up close. A lot of women look hot when they're on stage, especially holding a guitar. I had a Nancy Wilson/Heart and a Joan Jett t-shirt upstairs in my drawer that expertly illustrated that fact.

But none of that really mattered, because Nikki had a raspy, soulful voice that captured everybody in the room and held their attention. She wasn't Bonnie Raitt, but she wasn't far off. Same ballpark.

When she finished her set I turned around and ordered a second beer from the bartender.

"So there are no old timers around tonight?" I asked, when he brought it.

"Not that I saw, unless you count me."

He was joking, because he wasn't a day over 40.

"Can I get one of those?" a woman's voice asked from right behind me.

I turned and found myself looking into the steady gaze of Nikki Rialto.

"Oh," I said, smooth as ever, "wow, uh, sure, a Yazoo for the lady."

"Mind if I sit?" she asked.

"Not at all."

She took a stool right next to me and smiled. Up close you could see lines at the corners of her eyes and mouth that gave away her age, but Nikki was still hot. Especially with the damp t-shirt. Even the smell of her perspiration was heady.

She picked up her beer and said to me, "You're Auggie Velez, right?"

"That's me" I said. "How did you know?"

"I saw you on The Voice," she said, "and I've seen you play around town once or twice."

"I'm flattered you remember me."

She drank down half her beer, gratefully.

"Ah, I always need that after a set."

I knew what she meant. Your throat could get really hot and dry on stage.

"Hi, handsome," she said, smiling and extending her hand, "I'm Nikki."

"I'm Auggie, I said, shaking her hand.

"How come we've never played together, Auggie?" she asked.

"I don't know," I said. "I guess we gig in different circles."

She finished her beer, held the mug out to the bartender, then looked at me and said, "I wasn't talkin' about on stage."

CHAPTER 13

WHEN I WOKE up the next morning, it took me a minute to identify the woman beside me. Then I got it. We'd come upstairs, jammed a bit with my guitar collection, and then she asked if I minded if this "sweaty old broad" crawled all over me. I told her to be my guest.

She tasted of cigarettes, beer and sex. The latter two made it sexy. I managed to live with the former. Sometimes you've got to take the good with the bad, and there was a helluva lot of good. At that moment she rolled onto her back.

The morning light brought with it some indications of her age. Slight bags under the eyes, lines at the corners of her mouth were deeper, a little saggy bit under her chin. She worked out, though, which kept her looking about 35 from the neck down. She had good tennis ball sized tits that sagged only slightly, brown nipples that I had spent a lot of time on, a flat tummy, long, graceful legs.

She opened her eyes and caught me studying her.

"The harsh light of day," she said, covering her face with both hands.

I swiped her hands away and said, "Don't. I'm not seeing anything I didn't see last night."

She frowned. "Really?"

I nodded, put my hand flat on her belly.

"So you're ready to go again?" she asked.

"Oh yeah," I said moving my hand lower . . .

━━

I don't keep a lot of food in my place. In fact, I don't even have a stove that works. I do everything with a microwave or toaster. I was able to offer a variety of cereals, though. We sat across from each other, she with her Frosted Flakes and a banana, me with Rice Krispies, wand a handful of green grapes dropped in.

"I don't think I've ever known a man who lives alone and doesn't exist off frozen dinners."

"I eat out a lot, and I have lots of canned goods and fruit."

"You don't have a stove but you do have the microwave and a refrigerator. Why not frozen dinners?"

"I tried for a while, but never developed a taste. All I like is the frozen fried chicken."

"What about frozen pizza? It's convenient."

"I can call and have it delivered faster."

"Good point."

She was wearing my Joan Jett t-shirt. After she asked me for something to wear I pointed her to a chest of drawers. It didn't matter which drawer she opened, she'd find t-shirts. When she found the Jett she said Joan was a hero of hers.

"You have quite a collection here," she commented, before closing the drawer.

"I know, I should own some button down shirts, but . . ."

"You're not a button down guy."

"Right."

Over breakfast we talked guitars and music, until we got on the subject of what else we do."

"You're a private eye?" she asked.

"Yup."

"Are you workin' on somethin' now?" she asked, lowering her voice.

"I am," I said. "Right now I've been hired to find Hammer Dylan."

"Hammer!" she said. "I thought he was dead."

"Everyone agrees he's missing," I said. But everyone agrees he's dead."

"Wow," she said, "if he's not dead . . ." She shook her head.

"Did you know him?" I asked.

She hesitated, then said, "I did. I was fifteen years old when he deflowered me."

I gaped at her.

"He raped you?"

"It was only rape because he was thirty at the time and I was fifteen," she said. "To be fair, the sex was consensual, and I told him I was eighteen."

"When was that?"

"Two years before he disappeared."

"So when he vanished you were seventeen?"

She smiled.

"You gonna do the math?"

It took me a moment to realize she thought I was trying to figure out her age.

"No, no," I said, "that's not what I meant, at all. I've just been looking for people who knew Hammer. How well—I mean, what were you doing? Singing with him?"

"I was trying to break in," she said. "I heard he was playing in town—I'm from Detroit—and I knew somebody who worked at the venue. To make a long story short, I got in, I met him, I thought he liked me. I thought he was gonna help me break in."

"And?"

"He got me to his hotel room, fucked me, and left town the next day. I never saw him again."

"What did you do?"

"I focused on breaking into the music biz on my own."

"And you did."

"It took longer than I would've liked, but yeah."

"And how do you feel about Hammer?"

"Well," she said, "back then I wanted to kill him, but I got over it."

"You could've accused him of rape," I said. "The way things are going these days with Cosby and Weinstein, you still could."

"Not my style," she said. "What could I possibly prove forty-five years later?"

"Nobody else seems to be worried about proving their accusations," I said. "Why would you?"

———

After breakfast she put on her tank top and jeans and thanked me for everything.

"The breakfast," she said, "and a wonderful night." She kissed me on the cheek.

As I walked her to the door I said, "Who knows, maybe we can play together some night—I mean, a gig."

"Oh, I'm afraid not," she said, just before going out the door. "I make it a rule never to mix business with pleasure. I never sleep with any of my musicians. And now, well . . . we slept together."

"I get it," I said. "Thanks for a great time."

She put her hand on my arm and rubbed it.

"You understand," she said. "I'm so glad."

I watched her go down the stairs and out the door, figured the only time I'd ever see her again was on stage, somewhere. I'd just had a one-night stand with a 60 year old woman.

Yes, I did the math.

CHAPTER 14

I HAD two choices for the day: go and see Corky Barnes, or drive to Anthem. I chose Anthem.

The little town was several hundred miles south of Nashville. Once I got out of the city and away from the traffic, it was a pleasant ride. It was extra warm for May, and the April showers had done their job and brought the flowers.

When I reached the city limits there was a sign that said Anthem, pop. 496. Talk about small towns. I was surprised it even had its own post office.

From one end of town to the other was about a mile and a half. Obviously, it spread out to the east and west. But the town post office was easy to find, especially with the flag flying.

It was a small brick building with its own parking lot. There was a large truck backed up to the side door, either loading or unloading mail.

When I entered through the glass double doors I found myself in a lobby with rows of post office boxes. To the left were two doors, one glass leading to the front of the counter, and one Dutch door leading—I assumed—to the back.

I had the box number the Bannister Agency had been sending Hammer Dylan's checks to. I walked over, found it to be one of the smaller ones, just large enough for letter-sized envelopes.

I went through the glass door to the front counter, where there were no other customers at the moment. Behind the counter stood a slight, gray-haired man in his 50's.

"Can I help ya?" he asked.

"Maybe you can," I said. "My name's Velez, I'm a private investigator looking for whoever opened this P.O. box." I showed him the slip of paper with the number on it.

"You say you're a private eye?"

"That's right."

"Then you have no authority, no warrant or anythin'?"

"No, none of that," I said. "I'm just asking."

"Well, I can't tell you nothin' about the P.O. boxes. I ain't allowed."

"Are we talking not allowed, or not allowed . . . for free?" I asked.

"Mister, it don't matter how much you offer me, I need this job."

"How much does a postal clerk make, these days?" I asked.

"I'm not just a postal clerk," he said, "I'm the Postmaster, here."

"Postmaster?"

"That's right."

"And how many people work here?"

"Just me."

"So if I come back with a cop and he asks you, you'll answer him?"

"It he has a warrant."

"Where do I find the local cop?"

"You don't," the Postmaster said. "We ain't got one."

"No police in town?"

He shook his head.

"Why not?"

"The town don't wanna pay for one."

"What about the next town? Thy have police?"

"Oh, sure."

"So if I bring somebody from there—"

"—they got no jurisdiction here."

"So who does?"

The man shrugged. "State Police, I guess."

"And where's the nearest State Police station?"

"Sixty miles."

"Okay," I said, "Look . . . do you know who Hammer Dylan is?"

The man frowned. "I know who Hammer Dylan was. I like country music as much as the next guy."

"Okay, then, have you ever seen Hammer in here picking up mail from his P.O. box?"

The Postmaster looked shocked. "Hammer Dylan here? Hell, no! I'd've noticed somethin' like that!"

Of course, even if Hammer Dylan did have a P.O. box in this little nothing town, he could have somebody else picking up his mail for him.

"Listen," the Postmaster said, "I can tell you one thing, and I'll tell you for free."

"What's that?"

"Hammer Dylan ain't never been in this post office" the

man said, gravely, "and he ain't never lived in this town. If he did, believe me, I'd know."

"I appreciate that . . . what's your name?"

"Dennis."

"Dennis, can I leave you my card, just in case you think of something else you can tell me for free?"

"Sure," he said "why not?"

⸻

I sat in my car in the parking lot for a short time after. Did I expect Hammer Dylan to go walking by? Probably not. I was just trying to decide my next move. Should I stake the post office out and wait for somebody to pick up mail from that box? If I did, it might take days. But if I had somebody else do it . . . I didn't really use any other P.I.s in Nashville on my cases. If I needed help there was always Harley, but with the cancer, he was now unavailable. But he could always recommend someone to me, since he knew everybody in the business.

So I started my car, pulled out of the parking lot, and headed back to Nashville.

CHAPTER 15

THE RIDE to Anthem and back didn't take as long as I thought it would. So I no longer had any excuse not to go and see Corky Barnes at Starcade Records.

I did a job for Barnes last year. As partial payment he had promised to let me cut an album for Starcade. He reneged on that deal, and I hadn't spoken to him since. So I didn't bother to call ahead, thinking he wouldn't agree to see me. I simply went to the Starcade building on Music Row and presented myself to his receptionist.

"Can I help you?" She was cool, both in her demeanor and her dress. And by that I mean, this chick was ice cold. She was dressed to the nines in a tight fitting suit that showed off her figure and her legs. Her black hair was pulled back in a tight bun, and her skin was pale. I finally realized she looked like she had just walked off a Robert Palmer video. Her blue eyes fixed me with a gaze that I was sure had frozen many men in their tracks. It said "don't mess with me."

"My name's Auggie Velez," I said, "I'm here to see Corky."

"Do you have an appointment with Mr. Barnes?"

"No, I don't," I said, "but if you tell him it has to do with Hammer Dylan, I think he'll see me."

She started to say something, gave me a "yeah, sure" look, then picked up her phone.

"Have a seat," she said. "I'll check."

"Thank you."

I sat on a leather sofa across form her, so I was able to see the expressions on her face change until, finally, with a look of surprise, she hung up and said, "He'll see you."

"I know the way," I assured her.

"Nevertheless," she said, rising, "I'll have to walk you back."

"Fine."

In spite of the spurt of sexual harassment complaints in the media, I admired her tight butt as we walked down the hall to Corky's office.

She opened the door, allowed me to go in first, then said to another girl at a desk, "Mr. Velez to see Mr. Barnes."

"Thank you, Max."

As she closed the door behind me I looked at the second girl and said, "Max?"

"Her parents named her Maxine and she hates it, but he likes Max. Hi, we haven't met." She stood up, came around the desk and approached me. Except for the legs and the stilettos, she was the total opposite of Max. She wore a pretty bright blue dress that showed her toned arms and a hint of cleavage. Her auburn hair hung down past her shoulders, and the look she was giving me was, well, warm.

"I'm Lily," she said. "Mr. Barnes' new secretary."

"How new?" I asked, as we shook hands.

"Enough that I don't know your history with him," she said, "but long enough to know it probably isn't good."

"Nice call," I said.

"Well, he's waiting," she said. "Apparently, you said the magic words."

She led me to Corky's door, knocked, opened it, said, "Mr. Barnes," and then let me go in, closing it behind me.

Corky looked like a little Buddha sitting behind his big desk, rather than the tin pot dictator he really was. If anything, he'd put on weight since I'd last seen him.

"I don't have all day, Auggie," he said. "What's this about Hammer Dylan?"

"Nice to see you, too, Corky."

"Come on, man," he said, "we both know it ain't nice for either of us. Just get to the point."

I didn't know why he was so pissy. I was the aggrieved party in this relationship. I decided not to sit, not that he'd invited me to.

"Fine," I said, "I've been hired to find Hammer Dylan."

"Dylan's dead."

"Maybe."

"Are you sayin' he isn't dead?" he asked. "Because that would thrill me to no end. I'd sue him, of course, for breach of contract, but I'd still be thrilled."

"I don't know if he's dead or alive," I aid. "That's what I'm trying to find out."

"For who?"

"I can't say." I could've, but I didn't want to give Corky anything I didn't have to. "What can you tell me about a second album?"

"That myth?" he scoffed. "If there's a second album we sure don't have it. But if it exists, it's ours."

"What do you know about Hammer, Corky?"

"I know that when I bought this company thirty years ago, he was one of the reasons why. Of course, back then I thought he'd reappear and we'd do more albums. But Outlaw Dreams is still makin' money, which is all I care about."

"So if Hammer Dylan does show up, alive," I said, "you'll claim him."

"Claim him, sue him, kidnap him," Corky said, "Whatever I fuckin' have to do to get him to record for me. Does that answer your questions?"

"Some of them."

"Well," Corky said, "that's all the time I have." To illustrate that point he picked up his phone and asked, "Lily is my four o'clock here, yet?"

On my way out I heard Lily telling him, ". . . said he'll be here at four-fifteen."

"I have a four-fifteen, don't I?" Corky asked.

"Yes, sir," Lily said, "but I can move that to four-thirty—"

"You silly bitch," he said, "my four is at four, and my four- fifteen is at four fifteen. When my four gets here at four-fifteen, tell 'im to go fuck himself. And when my four-fifteen gets here, show him in. Do you understand?"

She looked at me, rolled her eyes and said, "Yes, sir."

CHAPTER 16

SOMETHING SOMEBODY SAID to me the night before resurfaced to me while I was leaving Starcade. I couldn't remember who said it but one of the old timers I interviewed said that Hammer Dylan often talked about attending his own funeral.

I got out my cell, called Carter Bannister's office and got his girl, Nancy.

"Hi, Auggie," she said. "What can I do for you?"

"Is he in?"

"Not yet. Can I help you with something?"

"Nancy, can you tell me if Hammer Dylan ever had a funeral?"

"Not that I know of," she said. "I mean, we don't know that he's really dead, do we?"

"No, we don't," I said. "What time will Carter be in?"

"Probably any minute."

"Okay, will you tell him I'm coming to see him."

"I will," she promised. "Um, bagels?"

"You got it."

When I entered the office with bagels and coffee Nancy gave me a big, pretty smile.

"Asiago cheese?" I asked.

"Yes, please!"

I left her a bagel and coffee and then went into Carter's office.

"Sesame, or poppy?" I asked.

"Poppy!"

I sat across from him and ate my buttered sesame bagel, drank my coffee.

"What's on your mind, Auggie?" Carter asked. "Nancy said you sounded excited this morning."

"Did she tell you what I asked her?"

"Yes," Carter said, "about a funeral for Hammer. There wasn't one that I know of. Why?"

"I was talking to some old timers, some of who knew him. One of them said that Hammer always talked about attending his own funeral."

"But there hasn't been one," Carter said, again.

"Right," I said, "but if we have one, maybe it'll draw him out."

"But a funeral? After all these years?"

"It doesn't have to be a funeral," I said. "What if we have a . . . a memorial. Invite some musicians to perform. Those who knew him, those who were influenced by him."

"And you think he'll come?"

"We'll play it up big, advertise it."

"And have, what, thousands of people come?"

"No, we'll have it at a small venue," I said, "the Bluebird maybe, with limited seating."

"How do we get these musicians to go along with it?" Carter asked.

"As far as they know, it's for real," I said, "so they'll be there if they want to be there."

"And why do we say we're doing this now?" he asked. "He disappeared forty-one years ago. That's not a milestone."

"I don't know, man," I said. "We'll have to figure that part out."

"And who's going to pay for this bash?" Carter asked.

"We'll sell tickets," I said. "It'll pay for itself."

"And hosted by who? He has no family."

"Hosted by you," I said, "his agent."

"But I'm not his agent—"

"Technically, you are," I said. "I mean, you're the Bannister Agency now, and he's still repped by the agency."

He chewed and gave it all some thought.

"Okay, this may work," he finally said. "Do you know the folks at the Bluebird?"

"I do."

"Do you think they'll go for it?"

"For the chance that Hammer Dylan might rise from the dead?" I asked. "I think so. What you should do is start working on a list of performers."

"I'll have Nancy get right on it," Carter said. "We'll start with members of Hammer's band who are still around."

I stood up, dropped my trash into his basket.

"I'll talk to the Bluebird crew and get back to you."

CHAPTER 17

THE BLUEBIRD GANG were all for it.

"How do you wanna do it, Auggie?" the manager asked.

"I don't know," I said, "how do you usually do memorials?"

"You can leave it up to us, then," he said. "We'll put it together real nice."

"Okay, good, that'll work."

"We'll just need a list of the performers, as well as a guest list."

"I'll get those to you as soon as we put them together."

"Fine," he said. "So, will you be playin'? You know we been tryin' to get you here."

"I'll be pretty busy with a few things, but if I get a chance, yeah, sure, why not? That'd be cool."

"That's great. We'll get started puttin' the event together. And I'll wait to hear from you on those lists."

"Okay." I promised, "I'll get them to you as soon as it's done. His agent's working on them."

We agreed to touch base again soon, and I left.

When I left the Bluebird my next stop was the Axe Man, to see Hoyt Bennett. But as I approached his store, I wondered if this was smart. I was going to clue him in on what we were doing, but had second thoughts. What if he *was* lying to me about knowing where Hammer was? And what if he *was* trying to steer me to Mississippi? Then letting him in on our memorial scam might be the same as letting Hammer in on it.

So I decided to play it the same with him as we were with other musicians who had known Hammer. Just let him know there was a memorial, and invite him to participate.

"Back so soon," Bennett said. "Wanna try that two-twenty five?"

"Not just yet. Hoyt," I said. "I wanted to fill you in some things."

I told him there was a memorial being planned for Hammer to be held at the Bluebird, and that they were inviting musicians to take part. I wondered if he'd be interested.

"In attendin', sure," he said, "but not playin'. It's been years since I played in front of a crowd. Nobody would wanna hear that."

"Well, if you change your mind I can make sure there's a spot open," I assured him.

"Thanks for thinkin' of me," he said. "But why a memorial now? Forty-one years later?"

I had been hoping he wasn't going to ask me that, since I still didn't have an answer.

"You know, I'll have to ask his agency that question," I said. "I'm not so sure, myself."

I told him I'd be in touch with the date and time, and left the Axe Man.

———

Something else occurred to me as I got back to my place. The first time I'd spoken to Hoyt Bennett he had commented that I was probably wondering how he could afford to carry the stock he had. Those guitars seemed way too expensive for a small store to stock. I wondered if he had a silent partner who had money?

When I got upstairs I called Elton's cell phone.

"Hang on!" he yelled. "I gotta find a quiet spot . . . okay, go ahead."

"Am I calling at a bad time?"

"I'm at a session," Elton said, "but I've got a few minutes."

"Who are you backing?" I asked.

"We're layin' down some tracks for Darius Rucker."

"Hootie? Is he there?"

"No," Elton said. "I'm disappointed, too. What's up?"

"The Axe Man."

"The store or Hoyt?"

"Both," I said. "Does he have a partner? A money man?"

"I've often thought so," Elton said, "otherwise how does he stay in business and carry such upscale stock ?"

"Do you know who it is?"

"No," Elton said, "but that shouldn't be hard to find out, should it?"

"Not if the names of the owners are registered," I said. "He might be getting the money off the books."

"He'd have to explain that, wouldn't he?"

"To somebody," I said, "like the IRS."

"You wouldn't . . ."

"You're right, I wouldn't," I said, "but I'll check into it."

I took a few minutes to tell Elton about the memorial.

"Well, phony or not, I'll be there," he said.

"So you don't have to buy a ticket I'll make sure you're on the bill."

"I'll just back somebody," he offered.

"Maybe Hootie!" I said, hopefully.

"Good-bye, dude. I gotta go back to work."

He hung up.

I made another call, to a contact I had at the Nashville Hall of Records. For the right price—and occasionally show tickets—she'd get me whatever I wanted.

"I'll look it up and get right back to you, Auggie," she said.

"Thanks, Dina. I appreciate it, and I'll show my appreciation in the usual way."

"I've got two words for you," she said. "Trace Atkins."

"You got it." I didn't know if I could get tickets, but I knew I was going to try my damndest.

CHAPTER 18

THE PLANS for the memorial moved forward very quickly.

Nancy called me and invited herself to lunch several days later. Carter had another appointment, but they had finally figured out their angle.

"So all you have to do is take me to lunch."

"You got it."

I had her meet me at Hattie B's Midtown location. They have two, the other one being on Charlotte Avenue. They specialize in fried chicken, served at different degrees of "hotness," including "Hot," "damn hot," and "shut the cluck up." It's owned by the father-and-son team of Nick Bishop Sr. and Nick Bishop, Jr.. I don't know them, but I love their chicken.

I made sure I got there first so Nancy wouldn't have to sit alone and wait. Yes, I'm a gentleman. And since I was buying a young lady lunch, I wore one of my dress bandanas on my bald head, and my Eric Clapton shirt.

They had picnic table seating, but I had chosen a 4 top so we'd have some comfort. There was a blackboard menu on the wall, and you have to grab a tray and go up and order your food, then carry it back.

When she arrived I stood up so she could see me, because the place was as busy as it always is. On some days, there's a line out the door and up the street. I tried to sit as close to the red chicken on the wall as I could so she'd spot me, and she did

"I love this place!" she said, joining me at the table.

"So you've been here?" I asked.

"I've been to the one in Charlotte."

"So then we don't need to look at the menu, do we?" I asked.

"No, sir!"

"I'll go up and get everything," I told her, "you just sit."

"It'll be my pleasure to let you serve me," she said.

I went up, got two trays, and filled them both with chicken, crinkle cut French fries, baked beans, cole slaw and pimento mac-and-cheese.

"Omigod," she said, when I came back balancing two trays.

"What?" I said, looking down at the table. "Not enough?"

"No, no," she said, "it's plenty. Sit down so we can start eating."

She was refreshing because she was a slender, pretty woman who literally ate with both hands.

We both spent some time putting a dent in the food, and then came up for air and looked at each other.

"Here," I said reaching over with a napkin and wiping the hoy chicken crumbs from the corners of her mouth.

"You're no better," she said and wiped mac and cheese from my chin.

After delivering the trays to the table I had made one

more trip to get us both a beer. After we both drank some, we were ready to talk while we continued to munch.

"So tell me," I said. "what's the angle of this memorial?"

"It was amazingly simple," she said. "This year Hammer would have been seventy-five years old."

"Or," I added, "if he's still alive he will be seventy-five years old. So it will be a memorial-cum-birthday party."

"Exactly," she said. "Of course, this is May and his birthday is August, but we're also going to talk about launching some new music in conjunction with his birthday."

"A new album?" I asked. "Not the second one."

"No," she said, "Carter's grandfather had some tapes of Hammer and some other musicians jamming, trying new things, working on some new songs."

"And he thinks he can make an album out of them?"

"Not a whole album, really, but he thinks he can put them out as downloads on iTunes."

"Is that for real?"

"Well . . . he hopes it is," she said, "unless you find Hammer first."

"When are we planning the memorial?"

"Today's Wednesday," she said. "We were thinking about this Saturday."

"How would you get the word out fast enough?"

"Email blasts, electronic ads, Facebook, Twitter . . . blah blah blah."

"Can you get it done that fast? I mean, we don't even have a line-up."

"Carter wanted me to ask you to make some calls, and get back to us by tomorrow."

"Tomorrow?"

"I'll be making calls all day today, and so will he," she

said. "Besides, it's not really real, right? If we say Tim and Faith are coming, they don't really have to show up."

I was thinking it was at least going to be real to the people who came to play.

"All right," I agreed, since this was basically my idea, "I'll make some calls."

"Thank you, Auggie." She sat back in her chair. "And thank you for this. I'm done."

There was still plenty of food on the table.

"I'll get some to-go boxes," I told her, "and then we can get going."

———

Outside she put her hand on my arm, kissed my cheek and said, "Thank you again door lunch. It was so good."

It was a different cheek kiss than Nikki's had been. This one didn't say, "This was a one-time thing and we'll probably never see each other again." No, this one lasted a little longer and included an arm squeeze.

Promising, right?

CHAPTER 19

I COULD HAVE GONE AROUND and talked to people, but that would've taken too long. For one thing, I would've had to wait until that night to catch musicians in clubs. So instead, I went home and started burning up my cell phone. By the time it got dark I had half-a-dozen names for Carter Bannister, both old timers who played with Hammer, and country stars who felt they owed something to him.

I called Carter's office and he answered the phone.

"I let Nancy go home," he told me. "What've you got for me?"

I gave him Mouth Organ and Bam-Bam, who both agreed to back anybody who showed up that night. Then I gave him 4 more names, all of which he recognized.

"What about Blake?" he asked.

"I called him, and he's busy with The Voice, otherwise he'd do it. What about you? Who'd you get?"

He named a couple of people who had also played with Hammer years ago. I wondered if he had called any who were under 70?

"Then I called some artists my grandfather knew," he said. "Reba and Dolly."

"You're kidding." Yes, I got excited.

"No," he said, "I called them, but they can't come."

Christ, that would've been phenomenal. I would've jumped on stage to play with them.

We ended up with a long list of possibilities out of the current crop of country artists—many of whom, I'm sure, didn't know or care about Hammer Dylan—and a list of second tier performers.

I was starting to have my doubts that this was going to work, and then I got an idea.

"Carter, why don't you do a press release or flier or whatever it is you're gonna do, mention a couple of recognizable names, and then say 'and many others.' That'll bring some ticket buyers in."

"And what if nobody comes, Auggie?" he asked. "Then what?"

"Somebody's gonna show up, Carter," I said "and we only need one."

"If Hammer shows up, looks through the front windows and doesn't see anybody he's probably just gonna leave," Carter said.

"Well, then, we'll make sure that's not what he sees."

━━

The thing about this memorial was that Hammer—if he was alive—had to believe it. I had the feeling the only way to achieve that was to get Hoyt Bennett to be there. And that could only happen if Hoyt truly didn't know where Hammer was, or even if he was alive.

Nancy had insisted I take the leftovers from Hattie B.'s

home with me. I was about to put them in the microwave when my cell phone sounded. It was Dina.

"I got that information you wanted," she said. "That store, the Axe Man, is owned by two men."

I knew it.

"Hoyt Bennett," she said, "and Winston Dylan."

Winston?

"Is that Hammer Dylan?" I asked.

"I don't know, Auggie," she said. "That's your department. You get those tickets for me?"

"You'll have 'em," I promised. That was when I decided to invite Trace Atkins to the memorial. And Dina.

I called Carter, hoping he hadn't left his office.

"What's up?" he asked.

"What's Hammer's first name?" I asked. "His given name."

"It's Winston. Why?"

"We might have a problem."

"Like what?"

"I'll let *you* know when I know for sure. Meanwhile, add Trace Atkins' name to the bill."

"You got him?"

"I'll get him," I said. "Don't worry."

As I hung up, I realized I'd made two promises about Trace Atkins I didn't know if I was going to be able to keep.

I put my leftovers back in the refrigerator, and wondered how long Hoyt kept the Axe Man open?

━━

It was getting dark when I got to the store, but the front door was still unlocked. Bennett looked at me as I entered.

"Now you got somethin' on your mind," he said. "I can

tell. Turn that sign around, wouldja? I was just about to close."

I turned the sign around so that it now said CLOSED to anyone on the outside.

"Come on in the back," he said. "You want coffee?"

"No," I said, as I followed him, "just some answers."

When we got to the back he poured himself a cup of coffee, added some whiskey this time, then faced me.

"Shoot."

"Winston Dylan is listed as a co-owner of this store," I said. "Is that Hammer?"

"It is."

"Why didn't you tell me that before?"

"I'm gonna give you the easiest answer to that."

"I didn't ask."

"You got it. But you should know, I listed him as co-owner, but he's not. He invested some money so I could operate the way I wanted, and carry the stock I wanted."

"So he hasn't been active here in all these years?"

"No, *sir*. I run the store alone, and my way."

"Okay," I said, "then listen. I need you at this memorial Saturday."

"Sure, I'll come."

"And I need to put your name on the bill, so that Hammer will see it."

"If he's alive."

"Right." I had stopped adding those words to the end of every sentence that mentioned him. I was pretty convinced that Hammer Dylan was alive.

CHAPTER 20

WE DECIDED that the Axe Man would be on the bill as a sponsor, and that way Hoyt Bennett's name would be on there, as well. If Hammer saw that, maybe it would draw him out.

I called Elton, asked him if he could bring some other musicians to the event, just to make sure we did have music. They could back whatever artists actually made the scene. I just had the feeling there were going to be a lot of no-shows.

Of course, the only "show" I was hoping for was Hammer, himself.

Over the course of the next two days I heard from Nancy that Shania, Miley and Brad Paisley were coming. But those were some major names to get on such short notice. I'd believe it when I saw it.

I had called Blake Shelton, who said he would've been there if he could. I also called Gretchen Wilson, because I had toured with her, but she wasn't in town.

And finally, Carter told me his grandfather had talked with Willie Nelson and Kris Kristofferson—two of the original outlaws—and they were going to come.

See what I mean? Big names, short notice. Maybe I'm just too cynical.

Friday morning I called Nancy and asked about fliers.

"You mean, paper fliers?" she asked.

"Unless you want to do plastic."

She laughed. "No, Auggie, you don't get it. We did electronic fliers."

"Electronic fliers," I said. "You can't staple those to telephone poles and tape them to windows."

"You can if you print them out."

"Well, I guess I don't need to." I said. "Do I?"

"Don't worry, Auggie," she said. "The word's out there. Carter's feeling very good about this."

"I'm glad one of us is."

"Come on, this was your idea."

"Yeah, I know, so how come I don't feel good about it?"

"Don't worry, Carter feels good enough for all of us!" she said, brightly.

After I hung up I wondered what made her so enthusiastic all the time? Were she and Carter a couple? I decided that didn't really matter to me.

I headed for the Bluebird to check out preparations.

———

Nancy's enthusiasm seemed to be contagious. Everyone at the Bluebird was running around energetically, getting ready for the evening's festivities. I couldn't understand why I had such a feeling of gloom and doom.

"Relax," the manager said to me. "Have a drink."

"Too early," I said.

"It was never too early for him," he said, pointing to my Kurt Cobain t-shirt.

"Maybe that's why he's no longer with us." I looked over at the bartender. "I'll have a cup of coffee."

I pulled up a stool while he poured me a cup and set it in front of me. It took me a minute to dredge up his name from all the bartenders I knew.

"You working tonight, Eddie'"" I asked, hoping I'd gotten it right.

"Wouldn't miss it," he said. "I heard Miley's gonna be here. She's sexy as hell."

"I hope you're right."

"Oh," he said, "she's sexy, all right.'

"No, I just meant about her bein—okay, never mind."

They weren't really open yet, so he continued prepping the bar.

The Bluebird didn't usually open during the day for lunch. They did two shows a night, and only operated around those two shows. On this night we were the 7:30 show. But that was hours away, and I couldn't just sit there and wait. I had no other cases to work, so I decided to go back home, pick up a guitar and work on a song I had started several weeks ago. I'd gotten stuck, and was letting it germinate in my head for a while. Maybe today something would break.

I said goodbye to the manager and bartender, told them I'd see them later, and left.

━━━

Word had gotten around Nashville that I was asking questions about Hammer Dylan. After all, I had hit a lot of clubs in my search for old timers who might have known him. The only reason I hadn't asked Willie Nelson or Kris Kristofferson about him was that I'm not privileged to have their phone numbers. If they showed up at the Bluebird later that night, would that mean they knew he was alive, or dead?

When I got home I tried putting Hammer Dylan and the memorial out of my head for a few hours. After all, I still had my own life to live, and that meant song writing. But I had only gotten about 20 minutes in when my cell phone sounded. I thought about letting it ring, but it might have been about Hammer.

"Hello?" I grabbed the phone right-handed, holding onto my Little Martin guitar with my left.

"Is this Auggie Velez?" The voice was dry, gruff, almost scratchy.

I put the guitar down.

"It is. Who's this?"

"Mr. Velez, I hear you're lookin' for me."

"I guess that would depend on who you are?" I set the Little Martin down.

"Yeah," the voice said. "This is Hammer Dylan."

"The dead Hammer Dylan?" I asked.

"I *was* considered dead for many years," the voice said, "but now, thanks to you, I'm very much alive—you sono-fabitch."

CHAPTER 21

"BEFORE WE START NAME CALLING," I said, "how do I know you're really Hammer Dylan?"

"Whataya want me to do?"

"Prove it."

"How do you suppose I kin do that?" he asked.

"You know about the memorial tonight at the Bluebird?"

"Ya mean my seventy-fifth birthday party?" he asked. "Like anybody wantsta celebrate turnin' seventy-five."

"Some people do," I said. "They're happy to be alive—but that's not what this is about."

"No," he said, "it's about you goin' all over town, askin' folks about me."

"And obviously somebody got back to you about it," I said. "Who was it? The Axe Man?"

"Hoyt?" the voice said. "Geez, I ain't heard from him since I gave him the money to open that place."

"So if not him, who?"

"It don't matter," the voice said. "What matters is that you stop."

"Look, I was hired to find you—or Hammer." I still wasn't ready to believe it was him. It could be a hoax.

"By who?"

I almost told him, but checked myself.

"If you want me to tell you that," I said, "then meet me."

"When?"

"Tonight."

"Where?"

"At the memorial."

"Geez—"

"Okay," I said, "come to The Bluebird after the memorial's over."

"If we're gonna talk tonight," he asked, "what's the point of the thing. You wanted to draw me out, so I'm out."

"We can't very well just cancel it. A lot of people are coming to honor you."

"Yeah, honor," he scoffed. "They're comin' to see if I'm really dead. Or if I'll rise from the dead."

"Look," I said, "I know you must've had a reason for wanting people to think you're dead. We can discuss that tonight."

"If I agree to come," he said, "will you not tell whoever hired you that you found me, until after we talk?"

"I can do that."

"Then okay," he said, "I'll see ya tonight."

"Wait!" I said. "How will I know you? I mean, it's been . . . years."

"I'll find you kid," he said, and broke the connection.

Maybe he would find me, but what would he want when he did? Was this guy on the level?

I picked up my Little Martin, but only to carry it across the room and set it on its stand. Why would he intend to do anything but talk to me? Certainly, nobody connected with my search for Hammer Dylan had any reason to do me any harm. At worst, this guy might just be an imposter. I'd probably be able to figure that out by handing him a guitar. The only problem with that solution was, everybody in Nashville played the guitar.

I got back to the Bluebird a couple of hours early, found Nancy there, but not Carter.

"He's picking up his grandfather," she told me.

"Carter senior is coming?" I asked, surprised.

"They both thought it was only right that he attend a memorial for his oldest client."

"Oldest is right," I said.

"Well, longest, anyway.," she said.

"You look pretty," I said. She was wearing jeans and a nice turquoise blouse. Simple, but effective.

"Thank you. You wore a dress t-shirt?"

Hey," I complained, "George Harrison *is* a dress t-shirt."

She put her hands out and said, "So-rry!" She looked around. "They let me in because I identified myself, but said they weren't open yet." I

"They only open during a show, and they didn't have an early one today so they could set up for this."

"And we start at seven-thirty?"

"Right."

"So when will they start letting people in?"

"Soon."

"And then we start looking for Hammer Dylan, right?"

"Right, and speaking of that, do you have any photos of him?"

"We had some old ones, and I loaded them onto my phone. Here, I'll text them to you."

She did that and I viewed them. Long hair, beard, head-band—looked like me before I decided to shave everything. Now the only similarity was the headband.

"Do you think you'll be able to recognize him forty-one years later?" she asked.

"Not a chance," I said. But I didn't have to, because he was going to find me. Or, at least, whoever it was I spoke to on the phone was.

She looked at the photos on her own phone.

"What if we just add grey, and wrinkles—"

"—we'd have Willie Nelson," I said. "Or Kristofferson."

"You're right," she said. "So how will we know him?"

"I'm hoping one of the old-timers attending will recognize him," I said, "or Carter Bannister the first will."

"Old-timers?" she asked. "Like who?"

"Like Bobby G-String, who just walked in," I said. "Excuse me. Since I invited him, I better greet him."

[⊐⊏]

For the next hour I was glad-handing the older musicians who showed up, many of whom I invited. Of course, Dolly and Reba didn't show, neither did Willie or Kris. And the bartender was disappointed that Miley didn't walk in, bare midriff and all.

Nikki Rialto showed up and performed on stage, which surprised me, since she'd told me she hated Hammer for raping her. But she was fantastic, and the crowd cheered. I didn't see her when she got off stage.

But enough musicians showed up to put on a show, and

people who bought tickets started to file in and fill the tables, chairs and bar stools.

Carter the Third showed up with Carter the First, and I got them installed at a table right up front.

"Keep looking around," I said to both Carters, "see if you recognize Hammer."

"That's what I'm here for," the older man said.

A few of the old-timers went over to say hello to the longtime agent, who smiled and was pleasant, whether he recognized them or not. But every time I looked over at Carter the First, he'd shake his head. At one point, Nancy sat down with the two men, but also kept looking over at me and shaking her head. I didn't know if it was because she didn't see anyone who could be Hammer Dylan, or she still didn't approve of my t-shirt.

There were plenty of men in the audience with cowboy hats, beards and long hair, some grey, some not. I finally decided to stop trying to guess. I'd just have to wait til after the show, when he came and found me.

And when Trace Atkins showed up and started singing, I really gave up.

CHAPTER 22

IT WAS A HELLUVA NIGHT.

After Trace Atkins finished and wished a happy birthday to Hammer Dylan, some of the old-timers got up and jammed with him. I would've loved it if somebody like Lucinda Williams or Tanya Tucker or Emmy Lou had shown up, but everybody seemed to have a good time.

I played a few numbers with Trace, and Elton Mott got up, as well. From the stage I noticed a guy sitting in the back, alone at a table. He had a black cowboy hat and dark glasses on, and a grey beard. I wondered if this was the fella I had spoken to on the phone, but didn't approach him during the festivities.

As the night finished off with a rendition of Hammer's "Outlaw Dreams"—I *had* to get in on that one—Carter Banister the Third stood up at the mike and introduced himself as "Hammer's agent." He thanked everyone for coming, and said that in the coming days he'd have some surprise announcements to make about Hammer Dylan's music.

People began to file out, musicians started packing their

gear, helped by a couple of Bluebird employees who acted as roadies for visiting bands. And then I noticed, in the back, that the black hat and dark glasses hadn't moved. I wondered if he was waiting for the place to empty out.

"Well?" Nancy said coming up to me. "Did you see him?"

"No."

"And nobody approached you?"

"Not yet."

"What do you mean, not yet? The night's over."

"There's a fella in the back I've been watching," I said. "I think it might be him."

"Where?" she said, swiveling her head. "Oh, the dark glasses?"

"Yeah, I think it might be him, but he's waiting—"

"Him?" Carter said, coming up on us. "Hammer? Where?"

"In the back," Nancy said. "With the dark glasses?"

"Is that him?"

"I'm waiting to see if he comes over to me—" I started, but Carter cut me off.

"Well, let's go ask him!" he said, and started across the room.

"Carter, wait—"

Nancy started after him, so I had nothing to do but follow.

I half expected the guy to get up and run, but by the time Carter reached him he still hadn't moved.

"Are you Hammer—" Carter stated, reaching out to grab the man's shoulder, but as he did the man simply fell sideways, off his chair and to the floor.

"Jesus!" Carter said. "I hardly touched him."

"Hang on," I said. "Back away!"

Reluctantly, Carter did. I moved forward, crouched over the man and checked for a pulse. When I looked up I caught Carter, Nancy, and a few other onlookers staring at me.

"We better call for the cops," I said. "This guy's dead."

CHAPTER 23

"THIS GUY'S HAMMER DYLAN?" Detective Lewis said, pointing at the dead man.

"I think they said they thought he might be, partner," Detective Hollinger said.

The place had been cleared out by the first police unit to arrive, and then Hollinger and Lewis showed up, just before the M.E. and his wagon. Now the medical examiner was standing off to one side, waiting for the word to remove the body. He'd already examined it.

"Okay, doc," Hollinger said, "what do we have, here?"

"He was stabbed to death, probably within the past hour," the M.E. said. "A long, thin blade, but easily hidden. It was expertly shoved between his ribs, right into his heart."

Hollinger turned and looked at me from beneath his red hair and behind his face full of freckles.

"Whataya got, private eye?"

"You know what this event was for, Detective?"

"Hammer Dylan's birthday, or something."

"Right. I was also supposed to meet a man here who claimed he was Hammer Dylan."

"This the guy?" Detective Lewis asked. He'd been a tired looking 50 when I first met him. Now, about a year later, he looked exhausted.

"I don't know," I said. "I thought it might be, but when we approached him, he was dead."

"How long was he here?" Hollinger asked.

"For the entire event," I said.

"Could he have been dead that whole time?" Hollinger asked.

"Possibly," I said. "I don't think I ever saw him move."

"Did you see him sit?" Lewis asked.

"Now that you mention it, no," I said. "One moment he was just there."

Hollinger and Lewis looked at each other.

"I guess he could've been killed and then put there," Lewis said. "The killer could've wanted him to blend in, and not be found until the end of the night."

"Or he could've been killed by anybody in here," Hollinger offered.

I thought about my client, Carter Bannister, who had reached him first. Could he have stuck him in that moment? Had he hired me to find Hammer Dylan so he could kill him?

"Okay, Doc," Hollinger said, "he's all yours." He looked at me. "We'll print the body, determine if it's Dylan or not."

"And let me know as soon as you do?"

"Tell me, Auggie," he said, "why were you lookin' for Hammer Dylan after all these years?"

"I was hired to find him."

"By who?" he asked, while the M.E. supervised the bagging of the body.

I looked around. The Carters were gone, along with

Nancy. Was there any reason to keep my client's name to myself? I didn't see one.

"Carter Bannister, of the Bannister Agency," I said. "He's Carter Bannister the Third. His grandfather was actually Hammer's agent, and now Carter wants to start the business up again. He wants me to find Hammer."

"That's fine," Hollinger said, "but where are they?"

"Carter's grandfather is very old, and he was upset by what happened here, so Carter took him home."

"And did you let any other potential suspects leave the premises?" Hollinger asked.

"Just Nancy," I said. "She works at the Bannister Agency."

"Could you gents excuse us?" the M.E. asked.

"Let's step over to the bar," Hollinger suggested.

The other attendees—the ones who hadn't already left before we found the body—were against the walls, having statements and contact information taken by the uniformed cops. I walked to the bar with Hollinger and his partner.

"Drinks?" the bartender asked.

"Coffee," Hollinger said.

"The same," Lewis said.

I nodded to the bartender to make it three.

Lewis looked around. "I've never been in here before."

"How long have you lived in Nashville?" I asked.

"My whole life."

"Never mind," Hollinger said. He was younger than his partner by at least a dozen years, yet seemed to be the man in charge. I guess it depended on whose name was on top when the call came in. Hollinger was probably the detective in charge.

The bartender laid out three cups of coffee.

"How many other potential suspects left before you found the body?" Hollister asked.

"A lot. They were filing out, and almost all gone."

"Great."

"But we have a list of everyone who was here."

"With addresses and phone numbers?"

"I think so," I said, "since they had to buy a ticket."

"So the dead guy had to buy a ticket," Lewis said.

I hesitated, then said, "I guess he could've snuck in."

"And so could the killer," Lewis said.

I stayed quiet.

"Okay," Hollinger said, "so lay it out for us, Auggie. Start to finish."

So I did, from day one, my visits to the old-timers, my drive to Anthem, the fact that the memorial was my idea to draw Hammer out, and finally the phone call setting up the meeting right there in The Bluebird.

"So do you think it was him?" Lewis asked.

"I don't know," I said. "He had the hat and the beard, and the wrinkles . . . it could be him—or somebody who was looking to scam me."

"I vote for the scam," Lewis said.

"Why's that?" Hollinger asked.

"I have his first album," Lewis said. "And I'm one of those who believes that he's dead."

"Well," Hollinger said, "we'll find out after we run his prints. Meanwhile, did you come across anybody who said they hated him?"

"A few," I said, thinking of Nikki Rialto, who had been there but was now among the missing. "From what I found out, he didn't get along with many people. If that's true, you're gonna have to count Willie and Kris Kristofferson among your suspects. Hank Williams, too."

"So a lot of people hated him," Hollinger said.

"A *lot*," I said.

"Were any of them here tonight?"

"I don't know," I said. "The ones I spoke to who didn't like him weren't here." And then I realized something, and Hollinger must have seen the realization on my face.

"What?" he asked. "What just popped into your head."

"There was one man I was waiting for tonight," explained, "who would've known if it was him or not."

"Who was that?"

"His name's Hoyt Bennett, he runs the Axe Man music store, which Hammer helped him start."

"The Axe Man?" Lewis asked.

"You've heard of it?" Hollinger asked.

"Yeah, it's on Music Row, somewhere."

"And you've been there," Hollinger said.

"No," Lewis said, "I've never had occasion to buy as guitar."

"Okay, so we'll talk to this Axe Man," Hollinger said. "Does Hammer Dylan have any family?"

"No," I said, "just his agent."

"Well, we'll need him to be I.D.'d," Hollinger said. "I guess that could be done by his agent, or this Axe Man."

"I can call Hoyt for you," I said.

"No need," Hollinger said. "I think I'll take my partner over there so he can finally see it."

"Will you let me know if you find out anything?" I asked. "I feel bad that this happened on my watch."

"You should—" Lewis started, but Hollinger cut him off.

"I'll let you know."

"Thanks."

As Hollinger and Lewis walked out I looked at the bartender and said, "Gimme a real drink, will ya?"

CHAPTER 24

TRUE TO HIS word Hollinger woke me the next morning. I checked the display to see who was calling and what time it was. I didn't recognize the number, and it was 9 a.m..

"I think you might want to get over here," he said, when I answered.

"Where?" I asked, trying to rub my face awake.

"The Axe Man."

He broke the connection before I could ask anything else. I left my place with a bad feeling in my stomach.

When I got to the Axe Man there were a couple of cars and a Coroner's van out front, which pretty much legitimized the way my stomach was feeling. It was like any minute it was going to bottom out. There was a cop blocking the front entrance.

"My name's Velez," I said. "Hollinger called me."

"He's inside." He stepped aside.

"Thanks."

"Damn shame," the cop said. "All them guitars."

That was when the bottom dropped out.

I entered the place and saw what he meant. Where there once was a wall display of guitars of different sizes, shapes and colors, now there was piles of wood and plastic splinters.

"Pretty bad, huh?" Hollinger asked, walking over.

"It's gotta be worse than this for you to call me," I said, "and for the Coroner to be here."

"You got that right," he said. "Come on."

He led me to the back room, which was crowded with activity: techs looking for prints or fibers, the M.E., his crew, Hollinger's partner, Lewis, and a few uniformed cops. On the floor was the man I knew was Hoyt Bennett.

"Can you I.D. him?" Hollinger asked.

Since he was lying on his back in a pool of blood it wasn't hard for me to see who he was.

"When I met him a few days ago he was Hoyt Bennett, otherwise known as the Axe Man."

"I thought that was just the name of the store," Lewis said.

"No, Hoyt played—not so much lately, but once upon a time. In fact, he even played with Hammer Dylan."

"You sure?" Hollinger asked.

"Well, that's what he told me."

"No," Hollinger said, "I mean, are you sure that this man isn't Hammer Dylan."

"Oh," I said, "are you telling me that the man who was killed last night wasn't Hammer?"

"We don't know," Hollinger said. "His prints didn't match anybody's in the system."

"Great," I said. "So it could be that Hammer was never printed? That means we'll never be able to I.D. him that way."

"Or the guy last night simply wasn't him," Hollinger said. "Now we'll check this guy's prints, and see if he's Hoyt Bennett, or Hammer Dylan."

"When was this one killed?" I asked.

"Last night," Hollinger said, "same way the other one was, blade strike right to the heart. There's no blood trail, so it seems like he was killed back here."

"Before or after?"

"The M.E. thinks this one was killed first, and the other guy second."

"That explains why Hoyt wasn't there last night."

"Was he supposed to be?"

"He was on the bill as a sponsor, but yeah, he was supposed to be there."

"Okay, so this guy had a connection to hammer Dylan. We don't know if the other guy did, but he was at the memorial."

"Which is enough of a connection," Lewis said. "We've got two murders that have to do with an old country singer who may or may not be dead."

"Auggie, we're gonna need everything you know," Hollinger said. "Everything you've found out during your search for him."

"Look," I said, "I don't have a problem with that, but let me talk to my client first, and then I'll come and see you."

Hollinger and Lewis exchanged a glance.

"I swear," I added.

"If you don't," Hollinger said, "we'll haul you in, Auggie."

"I get it," I said.

"Okay." Hollinger looked at the M.E.. "He's aLl yours, Doc."

"Bag 'im!" the doctor shouted.

"You mind if I have a look around?" I asked.

"As long as you tell us if you notice something we missed," Hollinger said.

"Definitely."

"Then go ahead."

The back room was still too crowded, so I went to the front. I stood there with the remnants of all those guitars at my feet. It probably made me a bad person, but it was here I felt like crying, not in the back room looking down at Hoyt Bennett's body. I saw pieces of the 225 and almost picked it up, except I probably would have been arrested for tampering with evidence, so I just stared.

I didn't notice anything Hollinger and Lewis had missed. I just saw what I felt were pieces of my life scattered about. I wondered if, after all was said and done, they'd let me come in and claim some of the pieces, salvage whatever could be salvaged. There were parts that could be reused, some necks, pickups, even turn pegs for tuning. There were necks with no bodies, bodies with no necks, things that just didn't need to be tossed away. I'd have to take it up with Hollinger, before he sent somebody in to clean up—if he was even thinking about that.

As if reading my mind he came up behind me. I broached the subject with him.

"Not up to me," he said. "But as of now, we don't know what family this guy had. We'll have to find out. If and when we do find an heir, I'll mention it to them, tell 'em you want to salvage some parts."

"I appreciate it."

"I appreciate you not touchin' anythin' while you were here," Hollinger said. "It must've been hard."

"You have no idea," I said, and left.

CHAPTER 25

I WENT TO SEE HARLEY.

Nurse Avery searched me from head-to-toe at the front door. I was going to have to apologize to Harley for not bringing him anything, this time, but I had come right from the Axe Man.

"Is there anything on the windowsill I should know about?" she asked.

"I don't know what you mean," I said.

She gave me a stern look and allowed me to pass.

"No hot dog?" Harley complained, as I walked in.

"Sorry, Harley, not today," I said. "This was a spur of the moment visit."

He shifted in bed to get comfortable, wincing as he did. If he weighed a 100 pounds I'd have been shocked. It was painful to see him like this, but what was my pain compared to his?

"I need some help on a case."

"Let me get my pants," he said, and then laughed a laugh that turned into a coughing fit. As Miss Avery appeared at the door he waved her away. There was a glass of water on the night table next to him. He took a sip from it.

"Okay, kid, tell me what you need."

"I need somebody to do some footwork for me."

"See," he said "this is why I've told you to get to know some of the other dicks in town."

"I know, I know," I said. My extra time was usually spent in sessions, or on the road. I didn't really have the time to get to know other detectives in town.

"Is this about Hammer Dylan?" he asked.

"Yeah," I said, "but now it's gone from that to two murders."

"What? Hey, come on, gimme details."

I relayed the whole thing to him and he listened intently.

"So you don't know for sure if one of the dead guys is Dylan."

"Right."

"And you think he might be in this town, Anthem? I never heard of the place."

"Me, neither. It's a smudge on the map, but it's got a Post Office."

"And you need somebody to stake it out and see who picks up mail from the p.o. box."

"Right, again."

"I got just the guy for ya," he said. "Take this down." He reeled off a phone number for me. "His name is Jesse Fogarty. He ain't real smart, but he'll do what you tell 'im to do, and he's a country music fan. You tell him this is about Dylan, he'll probably work for free."

"I'll have the agent pay him."

"I'll call 'im and give him a heads up that you'll be call-in', but I won't tell 'im nothin' about the case. That'll be up to you."

"Sounds good."

"Okay, then I got only one more thing to say to you."

"What's that?"

"Don't you fuckin' come here again without a hot dog."

"You got it, dude!"

On the way out I passed Nurse Avery, again seated in a chair, reading. She looked up at me and I expected to get another reaming from her, but all she did was cock her head, stare at me a minute, and then say, "I like the hat."

———

I left Harley's house without shaking his hand. We had never been demonstrative with each other, no hugging or high fives or butt pats between us, but we used to shake hands. Since his cancer had begun to eat him alive, I think he saw the look on my face the first time I felt its effect on him, right in my hand. After that day, we never shook hands again, and he just continued to waste away. I was hoping for news of the remission of his cancer, but it hadn't come yet, and I didn't know how much longer he'd last.

———

I wanted to call Jesse Fogarty right away, but knew I had to give Harley time to get to him. So I went to the Back Alley for what I thought was a well-deserved meal, and had with it what I knew was a well-deserved drink. Chicken and beer always did it for me. It was my comfort food.

I put my cell phone on the table within easy reach, wondering if I'd get another call from that voice, or if it had been silenced last night with one of the two murders. Could it have been Hoyt Bennett on the phone? I didn't think so. So maybe it was the man with the cowboy hat and dark glasses who had been killed at the Bluebird.

I hoped not.

I was almost willing the darn thing to ring before I finished my meal, but it never did.

"Anythin' else?" the waiter asked.

"Just the check, thanks."

He tore it off his pad and set it down. I grabbed my phone, settled up, and hit the street.

Broadway in Nashville was not anything like Broadway in New York, but I liked ours better. In New York you knew there were things going on behind closed doors. Shows, music, dancing. But in Nashville, the music found its way to the streets. You could walk down the street and hear it coming from different venues. Especially when you turned down my street, Printer's Row, where there were several clubs.

I resisted going into the Bourbon for another drink and instead, went up to my place. The music followed me up the stairs, but then I realized what I was hearing wasn't coming from the club, it was coming from behind my door.

Somebody was in my place, playing a guitar. I wondered if Nikki Rialto had decided to come back?

Rooster Cogburn was sitting on my sofa, strumming one of my Fenders. I mean, the guy could've walked out of the movie True Grit, and I mean the original, the John Wayne real deal movie, not the Jeff Bridges version.

"Hey!" he called out as I walked in. "I was wonderin' when you'd show."

"How did you get in here?" I asked.

"When you live to be my age, son, you learn lots of things. Getting' past locked doors is one of 'em."

"And the guitar?'

"Hey," he said, setting it aside, "I just had to pass the time while I waited."

He stood up, not as tall as the Duke, but an imposing figure with a prominent nose, and a beard, and no eye patch. He also had the belly that Wayne sported late in his career. And he had a worn Stetson on.

"Can I ask you what inspired you to get by my locked door" I asked.

"Well, friend, I hear you been lookin' for me."

I almost expected him to call me "Pilgrim."

Like most people—enough to make the record go double-platinum—I had seen the photo on the front of the OUTLAW DREAMS album. This man looked nothing like that. You'd not only have to pack on the years, but the pounds, as well.

"So you're telling me you're Hammer Dylan?"

"You got it, partner," he said. "And you're Auggie Velez, songwriter and private eye."

I stared at him for a few seconds, and then asked, "You want a beer?"

CHAPTER 26

"HOW DO I know you're really Hammer Dylan?" I asked.

He sat back down on the sofa when I gave him a bottle of Yazoo's Dos Perros.

"Son, why the hell would I claim to be if I wasn't?" he asked.

"Did you call me two nights ago and say you wanted to meet?"

"What? No."

"Well, somebody claiming to be you did," I said. "We were supposed to meet at the memorial at The Bluebird, but instead some guy showed up dead."

"Damn," he said. "Heart attack?"

"No, he was murdered," I said, "right after they killed Hoyt Bennett."

He stopped with the bottle halfway to his mouth.

"The Axe Man's dead?"

"That's right," I said, "killed the same way as the guy at The Bluebird, stabbed."

"Jesus, poor Hoyt."

"And that's not all. They wrecked his place, broke all the guitars into pieces."

His eyes widened. "Now that just ain't right."

"No, it's not," I agreed.

"All the guitars?"

"His whole stock," I said, "including a two twenty-five.."

"I don't know what that is, but it sounds like a shame," the man said. "You got some nice ones here, like this Little Martin." He picked up the one he had been strumming. "I kinda stick to my acoustic Fender."

"Same one you played on 'Outlaw Dreams?'" I asked.

"Same one."

"With the hole?"

He smiled, touched the Martin at the bottom, below the sound hole. "Right there." He smiled at me. "You testin' me, boy?"

"Maybe I am," I said. "Since yesterday I've come across two men who could be Hammer Dylan. They're both dead."

"Wait a minute," he said, setting the Little Martin aside. "You sayin' somebody's tryin' to kill me?"

"I'm saying that if you're Hammer Dylan, they're dead because I was looking for you."

"Who hired you?"

"Carter Bannister."

"Ol' Carter?"

"The Rhird," I said. "His grandson's taken over the agency, and you're his only client right now. If I can prove you're alive."

He smiled. "Now yer talkin' like you believe me."

"Let's just say I'm leaning that way."

"Well, how do I get ya to fall all the way over?" he asked.

"I don't know," I said. "Sing me a song."

"Aw man," he said, "my voice ain't what it used ta be, but all right."

He picked up my Little Martin and played the opening strains of "Outlaw Dreams," and then started singing.

I was shocked. It was him, right there on my sofa. And, if anything, the voice was better—deeper, richer, but undeniably Hammer Dylan. And the pickin'! I would've recognized that, anywhere.

I grabbed another guitar and started playing along with him, and before long was harmonizing with him, as well.

"Holy shit!" I said, when we were done.

"That bad?"

"Jesus Christ, no, that good!" I said. "Come on, Hammer..."

"Yer kiddin' me," he said, putting the guitar aide, again. "Sounds like an old gravel truck, to me."

"Jesus," I said, "Hammer Dylan, playing my guitar, singing in my home,.

"Now, calm down, son," he said. "This is just ol' Hammer, here. Nothin' to be thankin' Jesus about. Besides, ya weren't so bad your own self."

"But... you're not dead," I said. "Why aren't you dead? And why did you make people think you were dead?"

"Hold on, Bubba," he said, "ol' Hammer's been holed up here waitin' for you for hours. Can we get us somethin' ta eat?"

"I've got nothing here but cereal and fruit, but we can go around the corner—"

"Any way we could get something, ya know, like... brought in?"

"Delivered," I said "sure thing. What's your preference, Chinese, Italian..."

"How about just some good old American grub?" he asked.

I took out my cell phone and said, "Comin' up, Hammer."

CHAPTER 27

THERE WAS a local place I'd call every once in a while when I couldn't get out because I was sick or working on a song. I got them on the phone and ordered some Nashville hot chicken and French fries to be delivered as soon as possible. It wouldn't be as good as Hattie B's, but it would be okay.

"Workin' on a new song, Auggie?" the woman who took the order asked.

"I sure am."

"You gotta tell me when you're gonna play and sing for me, darling," she reminded me.

"You just tell me when your husband says it's okay, Lanie." Her husband owned the place I was ordering from. She always took my order, and always flirted. I'd never seen her, but she sounded sexy as hell.

"Aw, shucks," she said, "one night I'm gonna come up there and deliver this food myself."

"Twenty minutes," I told Hammer.

"Sounded like that little filly needed to be broke," Hammer said.

"That little filly's about fifty and has a husband," I said. "If I mess with her, I'm the one who's gonna get broke."

We both laughed, and I got us two more Yazoos.

———

We shot the shit for the 18 minutes it took the order to get there. He told me he was working on a new album called "Sweet Songs." Turns out he was living in a house in a holler near Anthem, paying a kid to check his box at the P.O..

"So the postmaster knows you live there?" I said.

"No, he has no idea," Hammer said. "The kid doesn't even know who I am."

"He doesn't look at the name on the mail?"

"Not if he wants to keep gettin' paid."

"And the name on the Post Office box?"

"Phony."

"And you got away with that? Didn't you have to show I.D.?"

"Well, it's not really phony," he said. "It's my real name. Harmon Davidoff."

"You're kidding?"

"No," he said, "whose name is really Hammer?"

"No, I mean . . . Harmon?"

"That's the last time I wanna hear you say it," he said.

"Got it." Davidoff? I thought.

"You know" he said, "I know who you are."

"You do?"

He nodded.

"I've heard you play a time or two."

"How?"

"I've managed to get some work from time to time," he said, "session work, background, whatever."

"And nobody recognized you?"

"Well," he said "I waited until I got older, put on some weight, got some wrinkles . . . I don't look like me anymore, do I?"

"Not hardly."

"There you go."

We were both seated on the sofa with the remnants of the chicken meal spread out on the coffee table in front of us. I hadn't expected to eat, since I had just come from the Back Alley, but when I smelled the chicken, I couldn't help it. of the eight pieces, he'd eaten six, and I had eaten two. We split the fries.

"Okay," I said, walking to the fridge for two more Yazoos. I handed him his, and remained standing. "Tell me why you disappeared all those years ago."

He put the beer on the table, wiped his hands on a napkin, picked the bottle up and sat back, sucking his teeth.

"So you think we're friends now?" he asked. "I'll tell you everythin'?"

"No," I said, "but you're here, aren't you? You obviously have something to say, and you've been waiting years to say it. So now's the time."

He drank half his beer down and then stared at me.

"You're good," he said. "I knew you were a good guitar player, and a halfway decent songwriter."

"Halfway decent?"

"But I didn't know if you were a good detective."

"So now you figure I am?"

"Like you said," he answered, "I got something to say, and it's time to say it."

"I'm all ears."

He studied me for a minute, and for a second I thought maybe he'd changed his mind, but then he sat forward.

"I need help finding my daughter."

CHAPTER 28

"WHAT?"

"She was born in nineteen seventy-five."

"The year you disappeared."

"Right."

"And she disappeared, too?"

"Right again."

I sat back down next to him.

"Tell me about it."

"There was a girl on the road, a one night stand," he said. "I was drunk, as usual—did you see that movie, 'Crazy Heart?'"

"Yeah, with Jeff Bridges," I said. "Everybody saw it. I liked it. It wasn't totally realistic, but—"

"That's how my life could've gone if I kept goin' the way I was," he said, cutting me off. "Real or not. I needed somethin' to make me stop drinkin'."

"And becoming a father did that?"

"No, I had already decided I needed to go somewhere and think. Then Lisa came to me, told me she was pregnant."

"And?"

"I freaked out. I was young, and the idea of being somebody's father never occurred to me."

"Did you ever see the baby?"

"No," he said, "Lisa told me it was a girl. That was it. She didn't want me to see her, was never going to tell the girl about me."

"And you never told anyone?"

"I didn't want anyone to know that I'd gotten a girl pregnant, and then ran. It was all too much for me, then. I—I did tell one person," he said, after some hesitation, "but that don't matter. Now I'm tellin' you."

"And now you want me to find her."

"Yeah, that's right."

"What's the point, Hammer?" I asked. "I mean, after all these years?"

"The point is I'm an old fart now, but I'm a father who ain't never seen his kid," he explained. "Lately, that's been weighing on me."

"But why let people think you're dead?"

"Hey," he said, "I never put the word out there that I was dead. People just started to think that when I went away, so . . . I let 'em."

"You invested in Hoyt's Axe Man store."

"I did," he said. "Hoyt was a good man, and I wanted to help him."

"So was he the only one you told?"

"I'm not gonna say, right now," Hammer said. "Auggie, I need this."

"Hammer," I said "I have a client, and I have a responsibility to him."

"Has he paid you?"

"Well," I said, "he's not exactly solvent, right now."

"I am," he said, "and I'll pay you right now." He took out a roll of bills that would've choked a horse. "Just tell me how much it's gonna take?"

"Put your money away, Hammer."

"Well, if you're not gonna help me, Bubba, at least lemme pay you for the chicken."

"I didn't say I'm not going to help you," I said. "Put the money away. I'm not taking anything for the chicken."

"And what about my daughter?"

"We can talk about that later," I said. "Right now I want to talk about you."

"What about me?"

"My client was not only interested in finding you, but your second album."

"Oh, that," he said, pulling a face.

"It exists?"

"Well, yeah, it exists," he said. "So does a third one, only I ain't recorded that one, yet."

"Holy crap," I said. "Two more Hammer Dylan albums?"

"Yes, sir, but nothin' like the first one," Hammer said. "I don't know if anybody would even like 'em."

"Trust me, they will," I said. "Why don't you let me put you together with Carter the Third—"

"Why would I trust him?" he asked. "He's just a kid."

"Why wouldn't you trust him?" I asked. "Is there something else going on you haven't told me about?"

"I'm just sayin'," he answered "he's wet behind the ears. Besides, if I give him a second album, Starcade is gonna go crazy. That Corky Barnes is a thief and a liar, and I don't want him gettin' his hands on it."

"Well, I can't blame you for that," I said, "but I'm sure Carter will have a lawyer for that."

"Look," Hammer said, "let's take care of one thing at a time. Find my daughter for me, and then I'll consider meetin' with the kid."

"No, I have a better idea. You don't have to pay me for my time, but if I do find your daughter, you will meet with Carter Three. Deal?" I put my hand out for him to shake.

He stood up and took it.

"Okay," he said, "you got a deal. But if I do cut another album, you gotta play on it."

"What?""

"You heard me," he said. "I don't know this new batch of musicians, or if any of my guys are still around. You have to play, and help me pick out the other guys."

I was stunned, and speechless for a moment, but finally managed to gurgle out, "It would be an honor."

"Don't be too sure," he said, releasing my hand. "You ain't heard none of the new songs, yet."

CHAPTER 29

I ASKED Hammer where he was staying.

"I got a place I crash when I'm in town," he said.

"And how often is that?"

"Just when I get the itch to hear some music, or play some, myself."

"And the guys you play with don't know who you are?"

"They're young," he said, "they just think I'm some old geezer who likes to pick."

"And you never run into any old guys who knows you?"

"Hell, they're old, I'm old, we don't recognize each other," he said.

"Well, you can stay here, if you want."

He raised his bushy eyebrows and looked around.

"That's temptin', Bubba," he said, "but I better stick with the place I got."

"You got a cell phone?"

"Hello, no," he said, "but I'll stay in touch with ya."

He started for the door.

"Hey, hold on there, partner," I called out.

"Yeah?"

I spread my arms.

"I don't know anything about your daughter or her mother," I said. "If I'm going to find her, I need some details."

He grinned sheepishly and said, "Sure, you do. I guess I thought you were a better private eye than you are."

He came back and sat on the sofa.

"Whataya need?"

───

We went through whatever details he had from 40 years ago. The woman's name was Lisa Martin. The incident took place after a show he did in Tulsa, Oklahoma. Months later, when he was in Denver for a show, she appeared and told him she was pregnant and expected nothing from him. He asked her to meet with him after the show, but she never appeared.

"That's it," he said. "Tulsa and Denver."

"Okay," I said, "describe Lisa to me."

"What for?" he asked. "She ain't gonna look like that, no more."

"Maybe not," I said, "but her daughter might look the way her mother looked then."

"I doubt it," he said. "She was a pretty woman, but the girl's got me as a father."

"Well," I offered, "maybe she took after her mother."

"I hope so, for her sake."

He said Lisa was in her early twenties, tall and slender, but with a good body and a mass of red hair. She wore a t-shirt and jeans. In some ways, the description reminded me of Nikki Rialto, so I decided to ask him . . .

"Do you remember Nikki Rialto?"

"Rialto?" he repeated. "Ain't she a performer?"

"She is, but she also told me that she knew you."

"From when?"

"She says you had sex with her when she was fifteen," I told him. "She's calling it rape."

"Nikki Rialto?" he said, again. "I don't remember—how old is she now?"

"Sixty."

"Look," he said, "I was drunk a lot on the road—drunk and high. If I had sex with her and she was fifteen, she probably looked eighteen."

"So you don't recall—"

"No," he said, "unless she had a different name, then."

"She probably did," I said. "I doubt her real name is Rialto."

"Did she say where it happened?"

"No," I said, "just that it did."

"How well do you know her?" he asked. "Could she be lyin'?"

"I don't know her that well," I said, leaving some parts out, "but why would she lie about it, all these years later?"

"I dunno, Bubba," he said, "why would she bring it up all these years later?"

"Let's just say we were talking," I said. "I was looking for people who said they knew you, and it came up."

"Well, if she claims she knew me, I didn't know her," Hammer said. "I've seen her photo, and her face doesn't ring any bells for me. But I'll tell you this. I've never raped anybody. Drunk or not, it just ain't in me. It ain't now, and it wasn't back then."

"Okay, Hammer," I said, "I get it."

He had gotten himself worked up, so now he stood and towered over me.

"You need anythin' else from me?" he asked.

"I think I've got enough to get started," I said. "You sure there's not some way I can get in touch with you, if I need you?"

"Don't worry," he said, "you'll hear from me every night. And hopefully you'll have some good news for me."

He started for the door, but stopped short, reached into his pocket and dropped a stack of cash on the kitchen table.

"That should be enough to get you started."

"I'm sure it is. Thanks." From where I stood it looked like rive grand. After he left and I counted it, I was exactly right.

"Are you gonna be lookin' for the bastard who killed Hoyt and wrecked his shop?"

"That's an active police case," I said. "I could lose my license by working on it."

"And the guy who got killed at The Bluebird?"

"Same thing."

"What'd he look like?"

"Old guy, dark glasses, black hat, long skinny face."

"Hmm. Sounds more like me than me," he said.

"You have a point," I said. "If he was going to try to convince me he was you, it was the old you—not the young one."

"I get it," Hammer said. "I'd like to know if the cops find out who he is. And I'd like to know who killed Hoyt."

"Detective Hollinger is supposed to keep me posted."

"How'd you work that out?"

"He's an okay guy," I said. "As long as I don't get in his way, or lie to him, he'll keep me informed."

"You gonna tell him about me?"

"I'm not telling anybody about you, until you give me the okay," I said. "That's our deal."

He nodded, repeated, "That's our deal," and left.

CHAPTER 30

I SAT, had another beer and went through the whole time I'd just spent with Hammer Dylan.

But was he really Hammer Dylan? I believed he was. Was he telling me the truth about everything? Probably not. Nobody ever does, why should he be any different? But was I going to help him? I was going to try. Why? Jesus, because he was Hammer Dylan!

"Okay," I said aloud, "we'll proceed assuming that he's Hammer Dylan."

I looked over at my Little Martin. Did I even dare play it again after Hammer had played it? I picked it up gingerly and carried it over to its stand and replaced it. After that I cleaned up the mess we had made of the chicken dinner. There were no leftovers, but I didn't want the remnants stinking the place up all night, so I tied the garbage bag shut and carried it downstairs.

I tossed my garbage in the Bourbon's dumpsters, which they kept behind the building. I only ever had one bag, so it didn't do any harm. I went out the back door, walked to the dumpster, lifted the lid and dropped the bag in.

Then somebody dropped the dumpster on my head . . .

⸻

. . . at least, that was what it felt like.

But let's be real. If someone had dropped a dumpster on my head I would've been dead. Instead, somebody had probably hit me with a more conventional item, like a blackjack, and then rolled me under the dumpster, where I woke up.

I crawled out from under, grateful that it hadn't rained in some time. Still, there was some garbage sticking to me as I sat up and pressed my back to the dumpster.

And then I went out again . . .

⸻

When I woke up the second time I was in the emergency room at St. Thomas West Hospital, looking up into some hellishly bright lights.

"What the hell—" I said, raising my hand to shield my eyes.

"Easy, buddy," a male voice said. Suddenly, a man's head was between me and the light. "I'm Doctor Lindstrom. You're in the emergency room with a pretty good bump on your head."

"Wha—" I touched my head and understood what he meant. "How did I get here?"

"Ambulance," he said. "Somebody who works at a Printer's Row restaurant found you out by the dumpster."

"The Bourbon," I said.

"That's right," he said. "You remember what you were doin' there?"

"Throwing out some garbage," I said. "I live upstairs."

"Okay," he said, "you sound like you've got all your marbles. Just let me have a look."

He had one of my eyes open, and then the other, peering into them.

"I don't think you're concussed," he said, "but not because somebody didn't try."

"Can I sit up?" I asked.

"I don't know," he said. "Can you?"

"Yeah."

"Show me."

He backed away and folded his arms. I worked my way to a seated position, withstood a bout of dizziness, and then slid off the table to my feet.

"Howzat?" I asked.

"Not bad."

I got a good look at him for the first time. He was a young emergency room doc, maybe early 30's, with dark hair and pale skin, like he worked all the time inside that hospital and never went out.

"Do I need a bandage or anything?" I asked.

"Nope, the skin's not broken," he said, "you just have a good lump. You'll have a headache, but just take some Tylenol and you should be all right."

"So I can go home?"

"You can," he said. "I've got a lot of people here in worse shape than you."

"Thanks, Doc."

"You're welcome, Mr. Velez."

"Did I tell you my name?"

"We got it out of your wallet," he said. "We didn't find anyone's name as a contact, though."

"That's okay," I said. "The only person I might've used as a contact has cancer, so he's unavailable."

"That's too bad." He took a piece of paper off his metal clipboard and handed it to me. "Just give this to the nurse at the front desk. We didn't find an insurance card, either, so . . ."

"Don't worry about it," I said. "I'll pay."

"They'll send you a bill," he assured me. "Just go home and get some rest."

"Can I sleep?" I asked. "I thought people with head injuries weren't supposed to go to sleep."

"You're not that bad," he assured me. "If you get nauseous and start to vomit, though, come back. Otherwise, you should be fine."

That didn't sound tremendously encouraging, but I said, "Okay, thanks, Doc."

I went out into the hall and started walking toward the front. I expected some dizziness, but made it without incident. I gave the nurse the slip of paper and she told me to take care of myself, and they'd bill me.

When I turned to go out the door I felt the dizziness, so I sat down on a bench before I fell down.

"Are you all right, sir?" the middle-aged nurse asked. "Do you want a doctor?"

"No, no, I'm fine," I said, holding my hand out to her, "but can you call me a cab?"

"A cab? Or Uber?" she asked.

"It doesn't really matter," I said. "Whatever number you have there."

"Okay," she said. "Just sit tight."

I sat for two hours before a car pulled up in front and a driver came inside.

CHAPTER 31

I CONSIDERED GOING into the Bourbon to ask some questions. I also thought about going to the police station to see Detective Hollinger, but I thought he might be home. So I left all of that for the next day.

I took some aspirin when I got home, because I don't believe in Ibuprofen and Tylenol and all that other stuff. Good old aspirin is enough for me. I touched the bump on the back of my head again, wondering what the point had been? If they were trying to warn me off, what were they warning me about? The only thing I was working on was Hammer Dylan. Who'd be warning me about that?

My head started to hurt again so I took some more aspirin and, since I wasn't feeling nauseous, went to bed.

When I woke up the next morning I didn't so much have a headache as my head simply hurt. It was sore, because somebody had apparently tried to send a message, when they could have done a lot worse. I was a sitting duck, and if they'd wanted me dead, I'd be dead.

So, what the hell?

I decided to go and have a talk with Hollinger. The only other person I might have talked to about last night was Harley, and I really didn't want to upset him, in his condition.

The front desk cop called the squad room and got Hollinger's okay to send me back.

"I know the way," I assured him.

As I entered, Hollinger stood at his desk, but Lewis wasn't around.

"Where's your partner?"

"He doesn't like our office coffee, so he went out to get some. Have a seat and tell me what's up? You look like you're gonna fall down."

"Knocked down is more like it," I said, sitting next to his desk.

I gave him the rundown of what had happened, leaving out the part about sharing hot chicken and my Little Martin with Hammer Dylan. After all, he wasn't looking for Hammer, he was looking for a killer.

"And you didn't see anyone?"

"I didn't see a thing," I said. "I was concentrating on getting my garbage into the damn dumpster, never suspecting I'd end up underneath it."

"Are you working on anything other than this Hammer Dylan case?" Hollinger asked.

"No, nothing," I said. "Until I got this bump, I was just going to spend time working at home on some new songs."

"Well," Hollinger said, "we can go down to the Bourbon and ask some questions, but if you didn't see anybody, it could have just been an attempted mugging."

"I'll tell you what," I said, "I can do that, myself." I stood up.

"How about lettin' us know if you find Hammer Dylan?" he asked, also standing. "I mean, just in case it's connected to what we're workin' on."

"Sure," I said, "why not? Speaking of which, you got any leads, yet?"

"No," Hollinger said. "We talked to other store owners in the area. A lot of them didn't know the Axe Man was there. One guy we talked to, though, said he thought that Bennett had an investor. We're tryin' to find out who that might've been. Any ideas?"

"No," I lied, "but if I get any, I'll let you know."

"I wish we could do more for you, Auggie," Hollinger said, "but we've got these two murders, and some other cases we've got on our plate."

"I get it," I assured him. "I do. I just wanted to let you know what happened."

On the way out the front door I passed Lewis, who had a take-out coffee in each hand. They were from The Frothy Monkey, not Starbucks. Monkey now had 5 locations in Nashville.

"Good taste," I said to him, pointing at the cups, and kept walking. Let Hollinger fill him in.

━━

I went back to Printer's Row. The Bourbon Street Blues and Boogie Bar didn't open until 11 AM, but I knew members of the staff would be inside, getting set up for the day, so I banged on the front door until somebody answered. It was one of the waiters, but he didn't know me anymore than I knew him.

"We're not open yet, man," he said, annoyed.

"I know that. Is the manager here?"

"Who wants ta know?" he demanded.

"I live upstairs."

He looked surprised. "Somebody lives upstairs?"

"Yeah, me. I want to see the manager, or Craig, the bartender."

"Craig ain't here. He's workin' nights. But the manager's here. I guess you can come in."

I slid past him and waited while he closed the door and locked it.

"You know where his office is, right?"

"Right. Thanks."

"I better not get fired for this."

"You won't." I put my hand out. "I'm Auggie, by the way."

"Billy," he said, while we shook. "Yeah, I've heard your name

around here."

I went to the manager's office found him sitting behind his desk, concentrating on some paperwork. I didn't have to interrupt him, though. When he saw me he stopped and smiled.

"Hey, you're up and about. How are you feelin'?"

"I've got a bump on my head, but that's about it," I said.

"Well, that's good," he said. "When I called nine-one-one I thought you were dead."

"You're the one who found me?"

"No," he said, "one of the busboys did that, but I called for help."

"Well, then I thank you both. Is he around?"

"No," he said, "tonight."

"I need to talk to him," I said, "see if he saw anything

last night."

"Like what?"

"Like the guy who hit me," I said. "Did you see anything?"

"No," he said, "but when Wes, the busboy, got me and we went back outside, nobody was there but you. Sitting with our back to the dumpster. How'd you end up like that?"

"When I woke up I was under the dumpster," I said. "I stayed awake just long enough to crawl out."

"So you didn't see anybody, either."

"Nope," I said. "I didn't see or hear anything. Whoever it was, they were quiet."

"You're lucky they didn't kill you. What's this about, anyway?"

"I don't know," I said. "That's the problem. It could've just been a mugging."

"Somebody waiting by the dumpsters to mug somebody?" he asked. "That doesn't sound right."

"No, it doesn't," I said.

"Did they take anything?"

"No," I said, "but then I didn't have anything with me. I was just throwing out my trash."

He sat back in his chair.

"Well," he said, "if there's anything I can do, let me know."

"Thanks. I think I'll come back tonight to talk to—Wes, was it?"

"Yeah," he said, "Wes, the busboy."

"Okay, cool," I said. "I'll see you tonight."

"Watch your back," he called as I left. "Nashville doesn't want to lose one of its best guitar players."

I waved my thanks and headed for the front door.

CHAPTER 32

I HAVE a laptop

I don't use it a lot.

Many of my music colleagues use them, and even write songs on them. On occasion I will use it for my investigations—like trying to find a woman who was born 40 years ago.

But first I had to talk to the P.I. Harley had recommended to me, Jesse Fogarty. Even thought I was 90% certain I had found Hammer Dylan, I decided to go ahead with my plan to have Fogarty watch the p.o. box. It might still be interesting to see who was collecting the mail from the box.

I went upstairs to my place, got a beer from the fridge and sat on the sofa with my cell phone. I dug out the slip of paper Harley had written the number on. The handwriting was shaky, which made me feel bad for him, again.

I punched in the number. A rough-edged man's voice answered and said, "Yeah?" in an annoyed tone.

"Jesse Fogarty?"

After a pause the voice asked, "Who wantsta know?"

"This is Auggie Velez," I said. "Harley Rayborn gave me your number."

"Oh, Harley, yeah, Jesus," he said, "poor Harley. Yeah, he called me about you. How are ya?"

"I'm good. Did I catch you at a bad time?"

"You got a job I'm gonna get paid for?" he asked.

"I do."

"Then it ain't a bad time. Only . . ."

"Only what?"

"Well, it ain't exactly a good time."

"When would be a good time?" I asked.

"Um . . . later tonight?"

"Sure," I said. "When and where?"

"You say."

"You know the Bourbon Boogie Bar on Printer's Tow?" I asked.

"Yeah, I do."

"Nine o'clock."

"I'll be there."

"How will I know you?" I asked.

"Easy, I'm as ugly as sin. How will I know you?"

"I'll be at the bar," I said. "I'm young, bald, but I'll be wearing a baseball cap that says "Music City.'"

"Bald?"

"As a cue ball. "

"I'll see ya tonight, then."

We broke the connection.

I spent a good portion of the afternoon on the laptop. I checked motor vehicle records for Nashville and Denver. Also, death records. Hammer had no idea what the girl's name was, so all I could check for was the mother. And all I had was her maiden name. If she'd gotten married during the ensuing years, I wouldn't find any obituaries, unless they also mentioned her maiden name.

I checked hospital records, arrest records. You can do all that stuff on the internet, you just have to know how. And if you don't know how, the internet can teach you, like it taught me.

I had to stop because my eyes were starting to burn, and I remembered why I never wanted to become a web surfer. I had also drank 3 bottles of beer while I was surfing. I needed to eat something, but it was too early to go to the Bourbon and I didn't want to go there until it was time to meet Jesse Fogarty. So I walked over to the Broadway Café for an early dinner. While I was eating my cell rang. It was Elton.

"I'm eating," I said. "You want to join me?"

"I was gonna ask you if you wanted to join me."

"Where?"

"Music Row."

"What's going on?"

"I'm in a session with some boys, and one of the guys suddenly got sick. I told them I knew a guitar man who could step right in."

"Is this for Hootie?" I asked.

"No," Elton said, "these are some new boys cuttin' their own stuff. They ain't bad. But they paid for this time, and if they have to cancel—"

"Say no more," I said. "I'll pick up a guitar And be right there."

"Just bring a Fender," Elton said. "If you need anythin' else, it'll be here."

"Sweet," I said, and hung up.

Playing and singing with Hammer Dylan had gotten my juices flowing, and I was looking forward to stepping in with Elton for whoever these new boys were.

⸻

Elton wasn't kidding about these boys being new. They were a good 10 years younger than him and me, but after a couple of songs I realized they were pretty good.

After one particular song we stopped and they asked us how we thought it sounded.

"It's missing something," I said.

"What?" their front man, Billy, asked.

"Falsetto," Elton said.

"That's it!" I agreed, "especially on the hook."

"Shit," Billy said, "that was Danny's strong point, the guy you're replacing."

Danny had come down with a sudden bad case of laryngitis, which had panicked the other band members until Elton called me. I was filling in on guitar, with some background vocals thrown it. All I had to do was learn the songs real quick.

"Well, Auggie's replaced him pretty good so far," Elton said. "Let him do the falsetto."

"You can do that?" Billy asked.

"I guess we're going to find out."

So he gave me a quick tutorial, and both Elton and I also had some suggestions about where to insert it.

"Okay," Billy said, "wanna try it?"

"Let's go."

Billy turned and signaled to the technicians in the booth, who didn't care how long we took, since they were on time and a half.

"One, two," Billy counted, "one, two, three, four . . .

— —

When we were done and everyone was packing up, the guys all thanked me and Billy gave me a big hug.

"When you said you could sing falsetto, man, we didn't expect Freddy Mercury."

I thought I sounded more like Frankie Valle on a bad day, but I said, "Thanks for the compliment."

"You cuttin' your own LPs, man?" he asked.

"Not these days."

"Well, if you ever want to," he said, "and you want some musicians, man, you let us know."

The other guys agreed, patted me on the back, and then we all filed out.

"Drink?" Elton asked, outside.

"No, I've got to get back," I said. "I was in the middle of some computer stuff, but this was great. I needed this kind of break. Thanks, Elton."

"Sure thing," he said. "You know you're my number one go to guy."

— —

By 9:30 PM I was done with the internet. I washed my face with cold water and then it was time for a drink.

It was a week night, but that didn't matter; the Bourbon was jumping. Craig the bartender was behind the bar.

"Hey," he said, "a little early for you tonight, ain't it?"

"I've got to talk to a couple of guys."

"Like who?"

"One is Wes, the busboy."

"Oh yeah," he said, "I heard they found you out by the dumpsters last night. Too much Yazoo?"

"No," I said, "but I'll start with one."

"Comin' up."

He drew the mug and brought it back.

"Is Wes here?" I asked.

"He should be in the kitchen."

I sipped the beer and set it down. "I'll be back for that."

"It'll be here," he assured me.

I left the bar and walked to the kitchen doors, dodged a waiter coming out with his arms full.

"Wes inside?" I asked.

"He's there," the man confirmed.

I made sure nobody else was coming out and went through the doors. I'd seen too many accidents in that doorway to just go rushing in. Waiters and cooks were dashing around the kitchen. There were a couple of guys lounging in a corner, probably waiting for some tables to bus.

"Is one of you Wes?" I asked.

They looked at each other, straightened up, and the one on the left said, "Uh, yeah, I am." He was young and scrawny. I put my hand out and he took it, hesitantly.

"I'm Auggie Velez. I want to thank you for what you did last night, dude, out back," I said. "By the dumpsters."

His face brightened and he pumped my hand.

"Oh, that was you? Well, sure, I didn't do much. I jus' found ya."

"Well, I appreciate it," I said, releasing his hand. "I was just wondering . . . can you tell me if you saw anything when you went out there?"

"Huh? Naw, jus' you."

"Didn't see anybody running away?" I asked. "Or anybody hanging around, earlier?"

"Naw, nobody," he said, shaking his head. "Sorry, man. I'd like to help."

"Okay, well, just wanted to say thanks."

"You're welcome."

I started away, then turned back when I thought of another question.

"What were you doing out there, anyway?" I asked him. "Dumping garbage?"

"Naw, I just went out for a smoke."

"Oh, okay." I could accept that. I waved and went back through the kitchen doors to the bar.

When I got to my stool my beer was still sitting there. I picked it up and took a drink.

"Want a cold one?" Craig asked.

"No, this is good."

"Find Wes?"

"Yeah, thanks."

"Who's the other guy you're lookin' for?"

"Nobody you know, "I said. "In fact, he's nobody I know. I'm just meeting a guy here—on business."

"Oh," he said, "well, lemme know if you need anything else."

He went off down the bar to serve two girls who looked very underage.

CHAPTER 33

I WAS STILL WORKING on the beer when a guy sidled up next to me.

"Buy a P.I. a drink?"

"Jesse?" I asked, turning my head.

"That's me."

He was right. I was looking at possibly the ugliest face I'd ever seen. And I've seen Steven Tyler, Keith Richards and Marilyn Manson up close.

"Auggie," I said, putting out my hand.

He shook it. I waved at Craig, asked, "What'll you have?"

"What you got there looks good," he said.

"Yazoo."

"Perfect."

I pointed to my beer and held up two fingers. Craig nodded and drew.

Jesse drank half of it down and smacked his lips.

"That hits the spot."

He looked like he was over 50, overweight, and over-tired. But he had Harley's endorsement, and that was good enough for me.

"So," Jesse said, "do we wanna talk about Harley, or whatever's on your mind?"

"There's no point in talking about Harley, is there?" I asked. "Let's just get to it."

"Fine with me."

"Do you know where Anthem is?"

"Is that a who, what or where?"

"Where," I said," A small town south of here. Four hundred people and its own post office."

"A smudge on the map," Jesse said. "What about it?"

"I need somebody to stake out the post office."

"For how long?"

"I'm not sure," I said. "There's a p.o. box I wanted watched. I need to know who collects mail from it."

"That could take a long time."

"Let's start with a week, and go from there," I said. "Is that okay?"

He shrugged, picked up his beer. "Fine with me."

"You got a car?"

"I can get one," he said. He finished his beer, put the empty mug on the bar. "Who am I lookin' for?"

That was a good question. If I had already found Hammer Dylan, who was I looking for in Anthem?

"I'm trying to find out if Hammer Dylan's still alive."

"Dylan? The country singer?"

"That's right," I said. "Apparently, his album is still drawing royalty checks, and they're being sent to the P.O. box in Anthem."

"So you're hoping it's Dylan, himself?"

"If he's still alive, yes," I said. "And I don't want it to be him, my client does."

"And who's that, or shouldn't I ask?"

"The Bannister Agency," I said. "They rep Dylan—well, they did in the old days."

"They sendin' him the checks?"

"Dylan's agent was Carter Bannister," I said. "He's sending the checks on. Carter Bannister the Third, the grandson, is the one who hired me."

"Tryin' to take over the family business?"

"Looks like he has his grandfather's blessing," I said. "The only one who wasn't thrilled about it was his mother."

"Well, okay," Jesse said. "Unless you've got something else to tell me, I'll get a good night's sleep and an early start tomorrow morning. You got a cell?"

"Yeah."

He took his out and entered my number, and I did the same.

"Anything else?"

Briefly, I told him about the murders.

"Just want you know everything," I finished.

"The murders might not be connected to Dylan, then?"

"No, they have to be."

"You workin' them?"

"The police are," I said. "I'm just working a missing persons case."

"Ah," he said, and knowingly laid his index finger against his nose.

"One last thing," I said. "I was putting my garbage out last night and somebody laid me out."

"Mugging? Or something to do with the case?"

"I don't know for sure," I said. "It was out back by the dumpster, so I doubt it was a mugging. Who'd wait out there to mug a waiter or a busboy?"

"Good point," Jesse said, "but if not a mugging, and not a warning, then what?"

"I don't know," I said, "but now you know everything I do." Almost.

"Anybody else have all this?"

"No," I said, "just you and me."

"And there's still some things only you know, right?"

"Uh, yeah, right, but—"

"That's okay," he said. "It's your case. I'll just mull over what you've told me, if that's okay."

"Yeah, that'd be great," I said. "Let me know if you think of anything I should do."

"I'm mostly a foot man," he said, "but I'll need something to do while I'm sitting on your P.O. box, so I'll give it some thought."

"Thanks."

"You want me to check in with you every day?"

"No," I said. "Only if you find out anything."

"You got it."

"And you'll only have to watch the post office until it closes."

"People can probably get into the lobby after closing to check their boxes," he replied. "I'll look into it."

As he walked away I called over the din of the live music, "We didn't discuss your fee!"

He waved, said, "I trust ya," and kept going.

CHAPTER 34

IT MAY HAVE BEEN a waste of money to have Jesse Fogarty sitting on the Anthem Post Office, but then, it wasn't my money. At least, I hoped it wouldn't be my money. I still wasn't sure how Carter Banister was going to pay me for my services, but Jesse didn't seem concerned with how much he was going to be paid. Hopefully, it would all come out even in the end.

When I got back up to my place after Jesse left, I was wondering what had happened to Hammer Dylan. He was supposed to check in with me, and hadn't. Did that mean he wasn't Hammer? He was just somebody who had gotten what he wanted from me? Whatever that was?

I made myself a pot of coffee, had just poured a cup when my cell sounded.

"Auggie?"

"Hammer," I said. "I thought I wasn't going to hear from you."

"I wasn't gonna call. I didn't think you'd have nothin' to tell me after just one day," the man said, "but then I figured, what the hell. You got anythin'?"

"No," I said, "I had a small problem, last night."

"What problem?"

"I was in the emergency room."

"What for?"

"Somebody tried to kill me." Making it sound worse than it was.

"Jesus, man, how?"

"Tried to take my head off," I said. "After you left I put out my garbage, and that's when it happened. I woke up in the hospital."

"And how are ya?"

"The doctor said I'm okay," I said. "Whoever it was messed the job up."

"Did it have somethin' to do with Hoyt's murder?"

"Why would you ask that?" I said. "Why not ask if it had something to do with you?"

"Me? Why would it have somethin' to do with me?"

"Because that's all I'm working on," I said. "You."

"Why the hell would anybody try to kill you because you're workin' for me?" he wondered. "Or because you're lookin' for me?"

"I don't know, Hammer. But I'm going to find out."

"Well," Hammer said, "don't forget what I hired you to do."

"I don't forget what any of my clients hire me to do, Hammer," I told him.

"You didn't tell the kid about me, did you?" he asked, quickly.

"No, not a word," I said. "Not yet."

"And ol' Carter?"

"He's not my client," I pointed out.

"Okay, then," he said, "I'm glad you're okay. I hope you find out who did it before they try again."

"Me, too, Hammer," I said "Me, too."

"I'll talk to ya tomorrow night," he said, and broke the connection.

———

I woke the next morning feeling guilty.

Carter Bannister Three was my client. He hired me to find out if Hammer Dylan was still alive, and to find him, if he was. I owed him whatever I found out. Yet, I also promised Hammer not to give him up yet. So which way did I go? With my original client or with the legendary Hammer Dylan? The only way I could make that decision was to admit that I still wasn't 100% sure he was Hammer. Once I was dead sure, then I could deliver my report to Carter Three.

But I still felt guilty. So I needed to do something to get that off my chest. I went to see Carter.

———

When I walked in the office Nancy looked up from her desk and smiled brightly.

"Well, hello," she greeted me.

"Is he in? I know I should've called but—"

"Never mind," she said. "We're always in to you. Hang on." She keyed her intercom. "Carter, Auggie's here."

"Well, don't keep 'im waitin' out there," Carter's voice said. "Send him in."

"You heard the man."

"Thanks, Nancy. Sorry, no bagels and coffee today, but I came on the spur of the moment."

"I forgive you."

I went into Carter's office. He stood up, but remained behind his desk.

"Auggie, my man!" he snapped. "What do you have for me? Any news? On the murder, I mean. I hope you found out that the victim wasn't Hammer."

"You'd have to check with the cops, Carter," I said. "I can't work that case. Or the other murder."

He frowned.

"What other murder? Who else got murdered?"

"Sorry, I thought you would have heard." I told him about the murder of the Axe Man, Hoyt Bennett.

"He was killed the same way as the man at The Bluebird."

"Jesus! What the hell is going on?"

"Again," I said, "you'd have to ask the cops in charge. Detectives Hollinger and Lewis."

"Okay," Carter said, "why don't you have a seat and tell me what you can?"

I pulled a chair over to his desk and we both sat.

"I have a man watching the post office in Anthem," I said.

"Anthem?"

"That's where you—or your grandfather and your mother—send Hammer's royalty checks."

"I didn't know that," he said. "If I did, I might've gone there, myself."

"It's just a post office box," I said. "I have a man sitting on it to see who picks up the mail."

"What if there is no mail?" he asked. "What if they haven't sent a check in a while?"

"That's a good question," I said. "I guess you'll have to ask your mother about that. Your grandfather said she's the one who handles the mail."

"I can't do that."

"Why not?"

"She doesn't talk to me."

"Again, why not?"

"Family stuff."

"Why not ask your grandfather?"

"Same answer."

"But he's letting you run the business, right?"

"Not really," Carter sad. "See, I own it, he doesn't."

"How's that?"

"He gave it to my father," he said, "and when he died, he left it to me."

"When was that?"

"About ten years ago," Carter answered. "I was too young to do anything with it then, but now I can."

"And he can't stop you."

"Right."

"But why did he agree to talk to me?"

Carter grinned. "I think he did that to piss off my mother."

"You know," I said, "I think we probably should have talked about this before now."

CHAPTER 35

"I DIDN'T THINK it was a big deal. It was just—like I said —family stuff."

"Family stuff is a very big deal," I said. "It can really mess things up. What else don't I know?"

"Nothing," he said. "I mean, there's nothing else to know. I don't get along with my mother, my grandfather tolerates me because he doesn't get along with her, either."

"Do you believe your grandfather knows where Hammer Dylan is?" I asked.

"I'm not sure, but I know one thing," he said. "He's not telling me."

"Which means he's not telling me, either."

"Right."

"Okay, what about Mom?"

"What about her?"

"She's been sending checks to the p.o. box in Anthem," I said. "Do you think she knows?"

"Listen," he said "if grandfather knows, he's not telling; if my mother knows, she's not telling—not even my grandfather. This is why I asked you to look for him."

"Hired me."

"What?"

"You hired me, you didn't ask me," I pointed out. "I'm not doing you a favor."

"No, no, of course not," he said. "Yes, of course I hired you."

"You just haven't paid me anything, yet."

"Well, no . . . I still don't have any money."

"Carter, do you have any clients?"

"You mean other than Hammer?"

"No," I said, "not other than Hammer. He's not your client, right now. I mean do you have any clients. At all?"

"Well . . . no."

"Then how do you intend to pay me?"

"I don't kn—you said, in the beginning, that we'd work that out."

"I know I did." I was still trying to justify keeping him in the dark about my meeting with Hammer--the man I now believed was Hammer Dylan.

"Well, is that still the case?" he asked. "We can work out the details of payment later?"

"Yes," I said, "yes, it is."

He looked relieved.

"Good. Well, thanks for bringing me up to date."

"Sure," I said. "I'll talk to you again when I know more."

I stood up and left. Nancy was still at her desk.

"Nancy," I said "what does he do all day?"

"Um, he works."

"But on what?" I said. "You have no clients."

"Is that what he told you?"

"Pretty much."

"Hmm. Well, he sits in there all day, makes calls, I think he takes breaks to play some Candy Crush on his phone."

"That doesn't bother you?"

"What?"

"That he might be sitting at his desk playing Candy Crush instead of working?"

"Everybody's got to take a break, some time." She shrugged. "As long as he pays me."

"But does he?"

"Does he what? Pay me?"

"Yes," I said, "does he pay you?"

"Of course he does, silly," she laughed. "Who in their right minds would work for free?"

"Yeah," I said. "Who?"

———

Maybe I shouldn't have been so understanding in the beginning, when it came to my fee, but it was too late to worry about that. The silver lining was, I no longer felt guilty about keeping things from my client. After all, Hammer was my client, too.

Then I realized I was in the same boat with Hammer, since he hadn't paid me a dime, either. But after all, he was Hammer Dylan. He'd touched my Little Martin and sang for me in my apartment. What more could I charge him? On top of everything else, he'd said I was a good guitar player.

Yup, all feelings of guilt were gone. Time to get on with it.

CHAPTER 36

HAVING SOLVED my personal dilemma regarding Carter Bannister III I had a new one: why would a man be looking for his daughter 40 years after her birth?

Hammer told me he'd looked for her before, with no success. I might've been so star struck once he'd played for me that I didn't ask the right questions. Like exactly what steps had he taken to find her? Had he used anyone to help him? But I wasn't going to be able to ask those questions until he called me, again. Hopefully that night.

So until then, I decided to go and see Carter's mother again, to ask when she had last sent a check. I probably should have asked her when I first got the address from her, but the woman projected a chill that I had wanted to get away from.

I could've called her, but I made myself drive out there, again. Very often you can get something out of someone in person that you can't get over the phone.

When she answered the door she brought that chill with her. But for some reason, when she saw it was me, she thawed, immediately. I figured it had something to do with the tall drink glass she was holding in her hand, which was only half full at that point.

"Mister Velez," she said, "how nice to see you again."

I almost said, "Really?" but instead I said, "I have a few more questions, if you have some time, Mrs. Bannister."

She hooked her forefinger into the neckline of her sundress and said, "Well, okay, but only if you promise to call me Vangie."

"You got it, Vangie," I said, surprised by the sudden thaw. "And I'm Auggie."

"Come on in, Auggie."

As we crossed the large, marble floored foyer I asked, "Is your father-in-law around, today?"

"I'm afraid he's out of commission, right now," she said. "Napping in his room. When he's worn out like this he can't stay upright."

"That's too bad," I said, as I followed her. The sundress she was wearing gave her a softer, very feminine look that took years off of her. She even seemed to be walking with a spring in her step, but that might have been the booze.

She took me to that same room with the French desk, then twirled to face me and asked, "Drink? I'm having another one."

"Sure," I said, "why not? But I'm driving, so don't gave me a big glass like you have."

She went to a pitcher, poured and brought me a tumbler filled with orange liquid.

"Mimosa," she said.

I sipped it, found it to be way more champagne than orange juice, but it wouldn't impair my driving.

"Thank you."

She filled her own glass, which easily held twice as much as mine.

"Cheers," she said, and I suddenly got it. With none of the men in her life around, she was much more relaxed, even flirtatious.

Maybe even more helpful.

"So," she said, as if reading my mind, "what can I do for you?"

"I suspect," I replied, "that when I was here last time I could have gotten more information if I had asked the eight questions."

She raised her eyebrows, bounced up and down on her toes and said, "I suspect you're right. So . . . ask."

"Do you know where Hammer Dylan is?"

She folded her arms, holding the drink in front of her, and rocked from side-to-side. "No."

"But you mail out his checks."

"I do."

"Do you know who cashes them?"

"No."

"Are they made out to Hammer?"

"No," she said "they're made out to cash. My father-in-law says that Hammer always wanted his checks made out to cash."

That wasn't helpful. It meant anyone could cash the checks.

"Do you know who picks up the mail at that P.O. box?"

"No, I don't." She sipped her drink, looked at mine. "You're not drinkin'."

I sipped it. I liked orange juice, but I really wasn't much of a champagne guy. I set the glass aside. She watched, but didn't comment.

"When was the last time you sent a check?" I asked.

"Not for a while," she said. "A few months."

"When will there be another one?"

"I guess that'll be up to Starcade Records."

Corky Barnes, I thought.

"I have an idea," I said.

"What's that?" she asked, waggling her eyebrows at me. "Will I like it?"

"Probably not," I said. "Can you send an envelope to that P.O. box for me?"

"With what in it?"

"I don't care," I said. "A blank sheet of paper."

She frowned. "Blank?"

"Yeah," I said. "I just need something to be put into that box."

"Oh, I see," she said. "And you'll be watching it to see who picks it up."

"Right."

Suddenly, the chill was back. She put her glass down with a bang, almost spilling it.

"I don't think so," she said. "And you probably should leave. I think I hear the old man waking up. He's going to be disoriented, and having you here will just confuse him even more."

I couldn't figure out what had flipped the switch on her.

"Okay, but the mail—"

"Why don't you just mail an envelope yourself?" she asked. "I won't show you out. I think you know your way to the door."

"Sure," I said. "That's actually a pretty good idea. I don't know why I didn't think of it myself."

Sometimes I know I'm a better musician than I am a detective.

CHAPTER 37

OF COURSE I knew I could mail an envelope myself. The question I wanted answered was, when had she last sent one? Since it had been months, I went home, addressed an envelope, put a blank piece of paper in it, then walked to the nearest mail box and dropped it in.

Simple.

Even though I was talking to a man I felt sure was Hammer Dylan, I still would've liked to see who was collecting his checks in Anthem. That would be for Jesse Fogarty to do, and I'd have to let him know what I did. I decided to text him on the spot, and he replied immediately that he'd be ready.

There wasn't much more I could do about the Hammer Dylan affair until I heard from Jesse. It was a matter of time before I'd have to tell Carter Bannister what I found. So I needed to move on to Hammer's problem—finding his daughter.

All I had to go on was the name Lisa Martin. She had met Hammer at a show in Tulsa, so I had to assume she was from there or, at least, from somewhere in Oklahoma. I wasn't finding anything out on line so I thought the next step was employing some good old fashioned shoe leather and going to Tulsa.

Before I went, though, I needed to find out if it was okay with Detective Hollinger for me to leave town. I called his number and he answered right away.

"Where are you going?" he replied, when I asked him.

"Tulsa."

"For how long?"

"Maybe a couple of days."

"I don't have a problem with that," Hollinger said. "Just keep me informed if you're going to be gone longer."

"Gotcha. Have you and your partner been able to identify the first victim?"

"Not yet," he said. "We got nothing back on prints, so he's not in the system."

"Any word on who killed Hoyt?"

"Nothing," he said. "Nobody in the area saw or heard anything. You'd think somebody trashing the store the way it was would raise a helluva ruckus, but we got nothing. How about you, you find Hammer Dylan, yet?"

"Not yet," I lied.

"You think he's in Tulsa?"

"I'm going there on a completely separate matter," I said, still lying.

"Well, just check in with me when you get back," he said. "And you'll have your cell with you, right?"

"Right."

"Keep it on."

"You got it."

We broke the connection. I was free to go to Tulsa and

see if I could locate Lisa Martin, or her daughter. Failing that, I'd probably have to head for Denver, but that would come later. I just hoped the venue Hammer had been playing when they met was still there.

CHAPTER 38

HMMMER'S five grand came in handy when I had to book a flight on short notice. I took Southwest Airlines into the St. Louis Hub and, after a two hour stopover, continued on to Tulsa International Airport.

I had the option of taking a cab or a bus to downtown Tulsa, which was about 5 miles southwest. I chose a cab, thinking it would be quicker.

I told the cab driver to take me to a downtown hotel.

"Holiday Inn okay?" he asked.

"Fine."

Along the way I asked him if he liked country music.

"Crazy about it," he said.

He was in his 60's, so I figured he'd remember Hammer Dylan. When I asked he got very enthusiastic.

"Oh hell, yeah," he said. "'Outlaw Dreams' was an amazing album. When Dylan disappeared—aw man, what a tragedy that was for country music."

"I heard he played here shortly before he went missing," I said.

"That's true. It was a helluva show."

"You were there?"

"I snuck out of my father's house to go see it."

"Then you could take me to that venue."

"I would," he said, "but it's gone."

"Gone?"

"They built the Tulsa Performing Arts Center, opened it in nineteen-seventy-seven with Ella Fitzgerald. And they tore down the place where Hammer played."

Then I'd flown all that way for nothing.

"You still wanna go to the Holiday Inn?" the driver asked. "You look like you lost your best friend."

"Yeah," I said, glumly, "keep going." I'd have to figure something else out.

━━

In my room at the Holliday Inn I checked out the honor bar, left all the booze and decided to go down the hall to a vending machine and just get a Coke.

If I had a number for Hammer I'd have called him and tried to get another lead I could follow while in Tulsa. Lisa Martin might have lived there—and might still live there—but I had no way of tracking her. Then it hit me. We were talking over 40 years ago. That meant she would have to be in her 60's, and would probably be on Social Security and Medicare. And once she was n those systems, they'd have her maiden name, not a married or legally changed name.

I had a contact my City Hall in Nashville, Dina, who did favors for me from time to time—the kind of favors that you paid for. But I didn't know if she'd be able to look up government records, like Social Security and Medicare. But I knew who did have contacts like that. I made the call.

"You're where?" Harley asked.

Lucky for me he kept his cell phone near his bed. It was the one thing his nurse didn't try to keep from him.

"Tulsa, Oklahoma."

"Jesus, why?"

I told him why I'd flown there and what I had found out during my cab ride.

"That sucks," he said. "Whataya need me for?"

"Do you still have your contacts?"

"Well, yeah," he said. "I'm bed ridden, I ain't dead—not yet, anyway. Whataya need?"

"Social Security and Medicare records on a woman named Lisa Martin."

"Is that her married name, or maiden name?"

"I don't know. It's the only name I've got."

"Okay, lemme see what I can do. What're you gonna do in the meantime?"

"Hammer is supposed to call me every night," I said. "I'll see if he can give me another lead to follow while I'm here. Otherwise I'll hop a flight back tomorrow."

"What kind of lead?"

"The only kind he might have and not realize," I said. "Pillow talk."

———

I'd had a few one night stands myself—in fact, one recently, with Nikki Rialto. Hammer and Lisa Martin must have exchanged words at some time during that night. There might be something he knew but didn't remember and I intended to pry it out of him.

So I was stuck in the Holiday Inn, lying on the bed, watching SportsCenter, waiting for my phone to ring. When it did, it woke me up.

I grabbed the cell of the nightstand, almost dropped it, juggled it and finally answered it.

"Yeah, hello?"

"Auggie, that you?" Hammer's voice asked. "You sound like shit, kid."

"Hammer!" I sat up straight. "I've been waiting for you to call. Guess I fell asleep."

"Where are you?"

"Tulsa."

He got excited.

"You're in Tulsa?" he asked. "Did you find her? Did you find my daughter?"

"No," I said, "right now I'm looking for Lisa, but there's a problem."

"What problem?"

"I've got no leads. I was going to check the venue where you played and met her, but it's gone."

"I could've told you that."

"Why didn't you?"

"You didn't ask."

"Okay, well, I'm asking you now," I said.

"For what?"

"A lead!"

"What kinda lead can I give ya?"

"You spent the night with the woman, Hammer."

"Yeah," he pointed out, "one night."

"There must've been talking," I said. "I mean, in addition to the drinking and fucking."

"And drugs."

"Jesus! Come on, Hammer, Give me something."

"Like what?"

"Something she said, something you guys did, something you saw . . ."

"You want me to tell ya what we did?"

"Not that!" I said. I rubbed my hand over my face, still trying to wake myself up. "Just think back to that night."

"Aw, for cryin' out loud, Auggie," he said, "it was a one night stand forty years ago."

My father used to say, "For cryin' out loud," which usually sounded like "For cryn' out loud." Nobody said it, anymore.

"Hammer," I said, "if I don't get a lead before morning I'm just gonna hop a flight back to Nashville. There's not much else I can do here."

"Okay, okay, wait a minute," Hammer said. "Gimme a sec."

"Take all night," I suggested. "Call me in the morning, before I check out."

"Yeah, okay."

"And have something for me," I told him.

"I'll think of somethin'," he promised. "Say, what happened to that place I played, anyway? I mean, did they put something else there in it's place?""

"Yeah, now they have a performing arts center."

"Fancy," he said. "I ain't played no fancy places. I played joints, bullrings, cowboy bars, but I never did play anyplace real fancy."

"You can play wherever you want today, Hammer," I said. "Just tell people you're alive and the offers will come rolling in. Believe me."

"Yeah, right," he said, "folks are just waitin' on an ol' codger like me to come back from the dead."

"I don't know about an 'ol' codger,'" I said, "but they're waiting for Hammer Dylan."

"Yeah, well, I can't think about that until I find my daughter. That is, until you find 'er."

"Hammer," I said, "I'm still confused about this daughter thing. I mean . . . after forty years? Why look for her now?"

"Do you have any kids, Auggie?"

"No, never did."

"Then maybe I can't explain this to you."

"Maybe not," I admitted. "Call me in the morning . . . with something!"

CHAPTER 39

MY CELL PHONE woke me again.

"What?"

"Auggie, it's me."

Hammer.

I checked the time.

Six a.m..

"What the hell," I said. "Do you know what time it is?"

"You told me to call you in the mornin'."

"Not at dawn!"

"Oh, sorry."

"Hang on." I looked around, saw a half-finished bottle of water on the night table. I grabbed it and drank it down, then lifted the phone. "Okay, what've you got?"

"A tattoo."

"You have a lot of tattoos, don't you?"

"Not me," he said, "her, Lisa. She had a tattoo."

"Okay, maybe that's something," I said. "Where was it?"

"On her butt," he said. "The right cheek, I think. I saw it while we were . . . you know, rollin' around."

"What was the tattoo of?"

"Me," he said.

"Your face on her butt?" I asked. "That's gotta be one in a million . . . doesn't it?"

"Not my face," he said, "a hammer."

"Oh," I said. "So . . . it was symbolically you."

"I guess."

"What kind of hammer was it? Like . . . from a hardware store?"

"No," he said, "it was bulkier than that. With a big head and long handle. Like the kind they use on a . . . chain gang! You know, bustin' rocks? And it had lightning bolts around it."

"So was it . . . like, Thor's hammer?"

"I don't know," he said. "Who's Thor?"

"Okay, the hammer with the lightning is unusual enough."

"So, whataya gonna do with this?"

"I'll check out some tattoo parlors," I said.

"Do they stay around this long? Tattoo parlors? I mean, it's been forty years."

"That's one of the things I'll find out," I said, "but you did it. You got me a lead. I think."

"Well, let me know what you find out," he said. "Go back to sleep now."

"Naw," I said, "I've got to get going. I'll have some breakfast down in the lobby and then start checking tattoo parlors in town. You want to give me a number to keep in touch?"

"Yeah," he said, "this one's good. It ain't a burner. I was already intendin' to give you my number."

"Okay, Hammer," I said. "I'll be in touch."

CHAPTER 40

BEFORE GOING down to the lobby in the morning I checked my cell phone for tattoo parlors in Tulsa. I was shocked at how many there were. It would take me forever to check them all. I was going to need help.

The Holiday Inn had a hell of a spread in the lobby. They made it available free from 6 to 10. I made do with some toast, bacon and coffee, then went to the front desk to ask a question.

"Can you direct me to the nearest tattoo parlors?"

The girl there stared at me and said, "I'm sorry, sir. I don't even know if Tulsa has any tattoo parlors."

"Okay, thanks."

I was just taking a chance. It was more likely I'd find out from a cab driver or bartender.

"Oh, wait!" she called, as I started to walk away.

"Yes?"

"We have vending machines."

I smiled. "I don't think I can get a tattoo from a vending machine."

She laughed, too, in a much prettier way than I ever could've.

"No, I just meant the vending machine man is here, filling the machines."

"And?"

"And he has a tattoo."

Ah, finally, the point. And a good one.

"What's your name?"

"Wendy."

"Thanks, Wendy. Do you know where he is now?"

"Not really, but the vending machines are on floors one, three and five."

"Is he still in the building?"

"His truck's still outside, so yes. In fact, he comes early enough to eat breakfast before he works."

"Thanks, I'll look in the breakfast room."

We couldn't see the room from where we were, so I walked back to it, stopped in the doorway to have a look. I saw a man in some sort of uniform sitting at a table, wolfing down his breakfast of eggs, bacon, waffles, and toast. He was a big, young guy, with an appetite to match his size.

I walked over to his table.

"Excuse me?"

He looked up.

"If you lost money in one of the machines, I'll get it for you later. Right now, I'm eating."

"Nope," I said, "didn't lose any money."

I saw the tattoo Wendy had spoken about, on his right forearm. It was colorful, a bit faded, and I couldn't tell what it was, but that didn't matter. I pointed at it.

"I'd like to know where you got that."

He frowned, then looked down at his arm.

"My tattoo?"

"Yes."

"Why?"

"I'm interested in tattoo parlors in town," I said. "I thought I could just look in my phone, but there seem to be a lot of 'em. I need someone to show me the best ones. And the oldest."

He laughed.

"You're right, there are a lot.:

"Anyway, where'd you get it?"

"At a place downtown. I can write the address down for you."

"That'd be great. Thanks."

I went to the front desk, got one of their pads of paper and a pen, and brought it back to Jack. That's what it said on his pocket: Jack.

He started writing, and kept writing. When he handed it back to me in looked like more than one address. In fact, there were two addresses, and two cross street locations.

"I wrote down four," he said. "They're the most popular ones. I've been to all of them. I don't know the exacts addresses, but you'll find 'em."

"So you have more than just that one?"

"I have eight," he said, "but this is the only one that shows."

"Can you tell me if any of these tattoo parlors have been around for, oh, forty years or so?"

He pointed.

"That one," he said. "And there's another one down by the docks, but I've never been there. I don't think anybody ever goes there."

"By the docks, huh?"

"Yeah," he said. "You look like you can take care of

yourself, but I still wouldn't go down there alone, if I was you."

"Thanks for the advice."

I started to walk away, but Jack spoke up, again.

"You lookin' to get your first tatt?" he asked. "You look like somebody who probably already has a few."

"Nope," I said, "I don't have any, and I'm not getting any." I decided to be truthful with him. "I'm a private detective, here in town on a case that involves a forty year old tattoo."

He sat back in his chair and stared at me.

"No way! You're a private eye?"

I looked around to see if anybody else heard him. Apparently they hadn't, or they were pretending they hadn't.

"I am."

"Hey, why don't you get a cup of coffee and siddown?" Jack suggested. "Man, I love the Mannix and Cannon reruns of METV. Maybe I can help ya?"

I considered it for a few seconds, then thought, why not? Harley had once told me that the solutions of some cases came when you least expected them, from the unlikeliest of places.

"Sure, why not? I need to have some breakfast, anyway."

I went and got a cup of coffee and a plate of food.

"So," Jack said, excitedly, "tell me about this forty year old tattoo?"

"You're really interested?"

"Hell, you bet. Nothin' ever happens in this town." He leaned forward. "So what's it about?"

"Hammer Dylan," I said. "It's about Hammer Dylan."

CHAPTER 41

I DIDN'T TELL him the whole story, but I told him enough.

"So it's a tattoo of a hammer," he said, "and it's supposed to mean Hammer Dylan?"

"That's what I've got."

"Wow, and it's from forty years ago? That's crazy."

I finished my coffee and my last bite of bacon.

"I better get going if I want to check all these places," I said.

"Can you wait?" he asked.

"For what?"

"I just have to fill these vending machines," he said, "and then I can go with you. Take you to those places."

"You don't have to. I can rent a car—"

"No, no, I want to," he said. "Besides, that one down by the docks—you need somebody to . . . to back you up."

I studied him for a long moment. He looked so . . . so eager. But he was a big guy, and tattoo parlors were not ice cream parlors.

"Okay," I said, "but how about I help you first, and then you help me."

"Crazy!" He jumped up out of his seat. "My name's Jack, by the way." He stuck out his hand.

"I figured," pointing to the name on his shirt. "I'm Auggie." We shook hands.

"Let's go, Auggie. I'll teach you how to fill a vending machine."

＝

You'd think filling a vending machine with candy, chips, pretzels and soda pop was easy. It's not. There are tricks to it, which Jack showed me, and formulas. You'd think you could just put Milky Ways here and Twix bars there, but you can't. It all has to be figured out.

"See," he said, at one point, "this is a candy bar, this is a cookie bar. They're not the same."

"I get it," I told him.

I didn't know if my helping him got the job done any faster, not when he felt he had to keep stopping to instruct me. I finally convinced him to let me take a cart up to the 5th floor while he did the 3rd. Before I finished he showed up, approved of what I had done so far, and watched me do the rest.

He slapped me on the back when I was done and said, "You could take my job, now, Auggie."

＝

The first two parlors he took me to were comparably new— one had opened 6 years ago, the other eight. Jack had gotten a tattoo at each.

Since I was with Jack, they were a little more receptive to me asking questions. Just because a man is tattooed and pierced doesn't mean he's a criminal, but both of the guys I spoke to were wary of me, thinking I might be a cop. It was Jack's presence that got them to ease up.

"We got a few hammer tatts," the first guy told me. He showed me a book full of tattoos, including several hammers, but none matched the one Hammer Dylan had described.

The outcome was the same at the second place.

The third parlor looked more promising. There was so much time hardened soot on the front window that I could barely see inside. If it wasn't 40 years old, it was damn close.

The lone man behind the counter wasn't 40, either. He looked closer to 80. The paint on his body was faded and limp, as his skin was pretty much sagging on his bones. He had spiky grey hair, a beard stubble to match, and two earrings—both in one ear.

"Hey, Jack," the old man said, leaning on the counter. "Back for the left one?"

I looked at Jack.

"Leg," he said, "left leg." He looked at the man. "No, Malachi, not yet. My friend here, he's lookin' for a certain tattoo."

"Is that right?" Malachi asked. "A guitar?"

"Why'd you say that?" I asked.

"The shirt," he said, "that's Brian May of Queen, ain't it?"

"It is. You know your guitarists."

"I've been around a long time," he said. "So what can I do for you?"

"I'm actually not looking for a tattoo for myself," I said. "I'm looking for one a girl got forty years ago."

"Forty years?" Malachi laughed.

"You were around then, weren't you?" I asked. "When Hammer Dylan came to town?"

He brightened, stood up straight.

"The Hammer Dylan concert! I was there, man. He was awesome. What a shame. Do you know where he is?"

"Isn't he dead?" Jack asked.

"Naw," Malachi said, "he's probably off somewhere with Elvis."

"Elvis?" I said.

"He ain't dead, neither," Malachi said.

"Uh-huh. This tattoo is of a hammer, with lightning bolts around it. But not a hardware hammer. More like a chain gang hammer. You know, the kind they use to break rocks?"

"A hammer, and lightning bolts," Malachi repeated, as if tasting the words

"Do you have a book I can look through?" I asked.

"No book."

"Then how do you keep track of your tattoos?"

"They're all up here."

The longer I looked at him the older he seemed. I wondered what would happen to all those tattoos if he suffered from Alzeimers.

Malachi seemed to drift off somewhere, and when he came back he said, "Nope."

"Nope what?"

"Nope, I never did that kind of tattoo."

"Were you doing tattoos back then?" I asked.

He pointed to a dirty sign on the wall behind him. 50 YEARS EXPERIENCE.

"Ah," I said.

"But I never did a tattoo like that," he said. "I did do

Thor's hammer, though. In fact, a bunch of them since the Avenger movies started comin' out."

"Well, that's way too recent," I said. "Do you know any where I might look next? Another place in town that's been around as long as you have?"

"There's only one other place," he said, "down on the docks. The Port of Catoosa."

I looked at Jack.

"You know where that is?" I asked. "Is that what you were telling me about?"

"Yeah, I know it."

I looked at Malachi.

"They've been around as long as you?"

He grinned. "That's where I got my start."

CHAPTER 42

THE PORT OF CATOOSA had some connection to the Arkansas River. Jack tried to explain it to me, but I wasn't putting the pieces together. Catoosa was apparently a city in itself, but inside of Tulsa. It was the largest port in Oklahoma, and one of the largest insland-river posts in the United States.

"Okay," I said, as he drove us there, "enough with the history lesson. Are we sure Malachi was telling the truth? He started there?"

"Well," Jack said, "the port first opened in Seventy-One, so it's old enough."

"And Malachi's memory is good?"

"Come on, Auggie," Jack said, "he might be old, but he's sharp as a tack."

"Just how old is he, anyway?"

"I don't know, almost eighty, I think."

"And you let him near you with a needle?"

"Look, after I got my first two tatts at those other places, I found Malachi. Now he does all my body art. He's got the steadiest hands in town."

"If you say so," I said. "I'm not a tattoo guy, but I don't know if I'd let him near me with a needle."

Jack agreed to forgo the history lesson, so I was able to do some thinking as we drove to the port. There wasn't another seat, and I had to stand and hold on for dear life while he rocketed along.

"If this doesn't pan out, are there any other parlors around?" I asked.

"Maybe a few, but none this old," Jack said. "This's gotta be it!" He was excited.

As we got out of the truck I said, "Just let me do all the talking, understand?"

"Sure, sure, I understand."

He led me to a street that was a block off the dock, and to a storefront that didn't look as old or grimy as Malachi's. But if Malachi got his start here, then it was older.

As we went inside I could hear the buzz of a needle going behind some curtained doorways. Behind the counter stood a man in his 30s.

"Help you fellas?" he asked, as we approached.

Jack started to speak, but then remembered what I told him and shut it.

"I'm looking for a tattoo," I told him.

"That's good," he said, smiling, "because we've got a lot here."

I looked around. The place was surprisingly clean, and even smelled . . . antiseptic.

"Is this parlor over fifty years old?" I asked.

"It is," he said. "My grandpa started it, then my pa, and when I took it over I did a major overhaul in the place."

"That explains it," I said. "It's too clean for a tattoo parlor."

"But we do good work," he promised. "What kind of tattoo are you interested in?"

"A hammer, with lightning bolts around it. But not a hardware hammer—"

"You mean like that?" He pointed to the wall behind him, and that was the first time I saw the tattoo hanging there, among others.

"That's it?" Jack asked me.

"It must be," I said.

"It's supposed to represent Hammer Dylan. Remember him?" the man asked.

"What's your name?"

"Desmond," he said. "Des."

"Des, I represent Hammer Dylan."

"What? I thought he was dead."

I changed my pitch.

"His estate, then," I said. "I represent his estate, and I'm looking for the woman who got that tattoo forty years ago."

"Huh," Des said, turning to look at the art. "I don't think I ever knew who got it."

"Her name was Lisa Martin, and she got it on her butt cheek," I told him.

"Oh." He brought his gaze back around to me. "Well, that means my grandpa did it."

"He did?"

"Any time a girl comes in here and wants some ink on her butt or tit, my grandpa does it."

"Don't you mean he did it?"

"No," Des said, "he does it. That's him back there." He pointed to the curtain.

"Do you think I could talk to your grandfather?"

"Sure," Des said, "like I said, he's behind the curtain. Go on back."

I walked over to the curtain with Jack behind me. When I opened it we found ourselves looking at a naked woman, lying on her stomach while a very old man worked on her butt with a needle. Coincidence, huh?

The man was so thin and bony, what was left of his skin covered with ink.

"Whoa," Jack said, but it wasn't out of admiration. The woman was overweight and even her folds of flesh had tattoos. Apparently, this was just another in a long line of them.

The grey-haired old gent working on her stopped, slid his goggles up onto his forehead and looked at us. His eyes were a startlingly grey.

"Help ya?"

"Yes," I said. "I'd like to talk to you about your Hammer Dylan tattoo."

"Holy shit!" he said, looking shocked. "That was a long time ago. I only did it that once. Now you want one?"

"Why do you have it up on your wall if you only did it once?" I asked.

"That's my dipshit grandson's idea," he said. "He wanted to put a whole bunch of my stuff on the wall behind the counter. I told 'im to do what he wants. The place is his, now."

This situation made me think of my client, and how his grandfather's business was his now, as well. More coincidence. The world is made up of them, and sometimes they come in real handy.

"Well, I'm glad it's up there. It told me I was in the right place."

"I'll have to finish with Maggie first."

"Maggie?"

He looked down at the naked woman.

"Oh, well, I'm sorry to interrupt you, but I don't want one, I just wanted to ask you about the girl who got the tattoo."

"That was a real long time ago," he said, "but I remember her. That was one of the finest asses I've ever worked on."

"I'm trying to find her," I said. "Do you know if she's still around? Or where she lives?"

"I'd have to check my records, but I might have a forty year old address for her."

"That'll do," I said.

"I'll take a look." He removed his goggles, set them aside and stood up from his stool.

"Uh, what about Maggie?" I asked.

"Oh, she'll keep," he said, looking down at her. "She's asleep."

"She sleeps through a tattoo?" I asked.

"As you can see," he said, "she's had a lot of 'em. It's old hat to her. Come on, the office is back here."

CHAPTER 43

JACK SAID he was familiar with the neighborhood.

"That's Eastside. Parts of it have been up-and-down," he said, "renovated, rundown, redone again. They just can't keep it up, though."

"This is such a long-shot," I said. "Who stays in the same house for forty years?"

"My parents," Jack said. "And my grandparents. They all stayed in one house all their lives."

Now I was having second thoughts, because my own parents had been in their house for over 40 years. Maybe this was all a good sign.

Jack took me down a street of rundown homes and pulled to a stop in front of one.

"This should be it," he said. "That's fourteen-fourteen there, so this's gotta be fourteen-sixteen."

"Let's find out," I said.

We got out of the truck and walked up to the front door. There was a 1-4-space-6 sign there, so we assumed another "1" had fallen off. I knocked.

"Nobody home?" Jack said.

"Not so fast."

I knocked again.

This time somebody answered the door. It was a woman with long grey hair, who looked the right age. If I didn't know she had to be in her 60s I would have guessed her 10 years younger.

"What?" she demanded. She was wearing a v-neck T-shirt, and shorts. She had very good legs for a woman her age, with a tattoo on each lovely calf.

"Are you Lisa Martin?"

She leaned against the door. "Who's askin'?"

"My name is Augustus Velez," I said. I had decided to play it straight when I found her. "I'm looking for your daughter."

"My daughter?"

"If you're Lisa Martin."

"What do you want with my daughter?"

"Her father is looking for her."

She laughed shortly. "Her father was Hammer Dylan, and he's dead."

"Not so much," I said. "He's alive and he wants to see her."

She stood up straight and stared at me. She wasn't wearing a bra, either she kept herself nice and firm, or her tits weren't real. Either way, Jack was staring at her hard nipples, and I was trying not to.

"Who the hell is that?" a man demanded from inside.

"Oh," I said, reacting to the new developments, "husband?"

"Boyfriend," she said, and slapped me on the chest. "He thinks I'm forty-five, so keep your mouth shut."

"Got it."

A large man in his 40s appeared behind her, wearing a

wife beater t-shirt that showed off some muscles. His hair was a mess, and I had a feeling I knew what we'd interrupted by banging on her door.

"It's just some business, Earl," she said. "I'll be in soon."

"Insurance," I told him.

Earl glared at both me and Jack, and then turned and went back inside.

"Thanks," she said. "It's gettin' harder and harder for an old broad like me to keep 'em around."

"You're not so old," Jack said.

"You're sweet," she said, "but I'm sixty."

"Jesus," Jack said, "you look great."

"Well, I work out," she said, and then stuck her chest out and said, "and these are only a few years old."

"So you are Lisa Martin?"

"I am," she said. "What's Hammer want."

"He wants to see her."

"After all this time? Why?"

"I think he's feeling his age," I said.

"And where's he been all this time?"

"He still has to explain that to me, too," I said.

She bit her lip. "I don't know why I should tell you anythin'."

"There might be some money in it," I improvised.

"How much?" she asked, suddenly interested.

"I don't know, for sure."

"Enough to make a difference?"

"Maybe—but first I need to know you're the right Lisa Martin."

"I've had three other names since Martin, but it's my maiden name. What kinda proof do you need?"

"Well," I said, "we used your tattoo to track you down."

"That was my next question," she said. "About how you found me. The tattoo, huh?"

I nodded. "The hammer."

"Stupid thing for me to do, but it made sense at the time."

"Can you show it to me?"

She raised her eyebrow and smiled.

"You know where it is?"

"Yes," I said. "I only need to see it for a minute, and I can send Jack back to the truck."

"Hey!" Jack objected.

"No, that's okay," she said. "He can look. But it's gotta be quick before Earl comes back."

"Right."

She stepped outside and closed the door behind her. Then she turned, bent over, slid her thumbs into the waist band of her shorts, and pulled them down so that her entire ass was exposed.

Sure enough, there was the hammer with lightning bolts around it.

"Satisfied?" she asked.

"Oh yeah," Jack breathed, admiring the way one of the lightning bolts pointed right at the crack of her ass. Even more, we could see that she waxed—everything.

She pulled the shorts up and turned around.

"What's next?"

"Where's your daughter?" I asked. "I suppose we'd better see if she even wants to meet him."

"My daughter's a woman in her forties," Lisa said, keeping her voice low. "She has a home and career of her own."

"Husband?"

"No," she said, "she never got married."

"If she looks anything like you," Jack said, "I'll marry 'er."

Lisa smiled again. "You're sweet, but my daughter is a lesbian."

"Oh." Jack sounded disappointed.

"And she does look like me," she added, "thank God."

"Does she know Hammer's her dad?" I asked.

"No," Lisa said, "I never told her. But I will, especially if there's money involved."

"I'll have to talk to Hammer about that."

"Okay," she said. "You talk to him and get back to me. If we have a deal, I'll tell you where to find Leanne."

"Lisa!"

"I'm comin'!" she shouted, then looked at me. "He's impatient. Hopefully, when you come back he won't be here." She raised her eyebrows. "Then we could get better acquainted."

She went back inside before I could answer. She was an attractive woman, but I had already had a one night stand with a 60 year old woman, recently.

"What now?" Jack asked.

"You can take me back to the Holiday Inn."

CHAPTER 44

I HAD Jack drop me in front of the motel.

"What are we gonna do now?" Jack asked.

"You're done," I said. "Thanks for your help. Now I've got to wait to hear from my client."

"Hammer Dylan?"

"That's right."

"Is he really Hammer Dylan?" Jack said. "*The* Hammer Dylan?"

"That's something else I'm still trying to confirm," I admitted.

"Can't I help?"

"For that I've got to go back to Nashville," I said. "Right now I'm just going to sit in my room."

"What about dinner?"

"There's some take-out menus in the room," I said. "I'll do that."

"But I can take you—"

"Jack," I said, trying to let him down easy, "I appreciate all the help, but we're done for now."

"For now?" Jack seized on that. "So I can come back tomorrow?"

Not knowing if I'd need a driver I said, "Let's see what tomorrow brings, okay?"

"Sure, sure thing, Auggie," Jack said. "Thanks for lettin' me tag along today."

I got out of the truck and walked into the Holiday Inn lobby. There were coffee urns set up for guests, so I grabbed a cup—and a cookie—and took them to my room.

I sat in the armchair by the window, drank my coffee, ate my cookie, and wondered why I was seeing so many fine 60 year old bare butts, lately? First Nikki Rialto, and now Lisa Martin, two women who had kept themselves in pretty damn good condition. And two women who had slept with Hammer Dylan.

I thought to check my cell as I tossed my empty coffee cup, before looking at the take-out menus in the room. I saw that I had missed two calls. Both were Nashville numbers, but I only recognized one, because it was Detective Hollinger's. I didn't know the other, but that was the one that left a message.

"Auggie, it's Nikki . . . Nikki Rialto. I need your help. The police have arrested me for the murder at The Bluebird. They think I thought he was Hammer Dylan. Did you tell them what I told you—I—I didn't know who else to call . . ."

And she hung up.

What the hell, was all I could think. Was this what Hollinger was calling me about, too? There was only one way to find out.

I called his number.

"You were supposed to check in with me," Hollinger said.

"I haven't even been here one full day," I said.

"Well, a lot has happened," he said.

"I know. You made an arrest—Nikki Rialto. Why?"

"Her one phone call was to you," he said. "I found that curious."

"I missed the call, like I missed yours, only she left a message. What the hell, Hollinger? Why arrest her?"

"Because she hates Hammer Dylan."

"Did you identify the body as his?"

"No, but she was there that night at The Bluebird, and she thought it was him. So she killed him."

"Who told you she hated him?"

"I have a source. Now why did she call you?"

"Well, for one thing, she thinks it was me who told you. Second, she didn't know who else to call."

"How do you know her?"

"We're in the same business."

"Murder?"

"Music."

"So what're you going to do now?"

"Now . . . what do you mean?"

"Now that she called you."

"I'll get her a lawyer."

"Well, all I've got to say is, get her a good one. When are you coming back?"

"Probably tomorrow."

"Check in with me when you get back. Understand?

"I understand."

"Make sure you do!"

He hung up before I could get the last word.

I tried the number Hammer had called from last, but he didn't answer. So I used the phone to order a pizza. I'd just have to wait for him to call me.

. . .

The phone rang again just as there was a knock. I picked it up off the bed and took it to the door with me. I had been surfing through channels on the cable and finding nothing to watch. I actually started to think about renting a movie.

"Auggie, it's Hammer."

"Finally," I said, "I've been waiting for you to call."

"Somethin' happen?"

"Yes," I said "I found her."

"You found my daughter?"

"No," I said, "but I found Lisa Martin."

"That's great!" he said. "How does she look?"

"She looks great," I said. "She's probably about sixty, and has a much younger boyfriend."

"Well then, somethin's changed," he said. "Back when I knew her she liked older men."

"Did you know how old she was when you got her pregnant?" I asked.

"She told me she was over eighteen."

"The same thing Nikki told you, right?"

"Nikki?"

"Rialto," I said, "Nikki Rialto, the woman who says you raped her."

The pizza delivery guy's eyes got wide, so I paid him, tipped him big and sent him on his way.

"Hey," he said, "I ain't never raped anybody! Why are you bringin' her up, anyway?"

"She just got arrested for murdering you," I said.

"But I ain't dead."

"Well, you might have to come right out and prove that," I said. "Meanwhile, the cops think the man killed at The Bluebird might be you, and that she killed you."

There was a long silence on the other end, while I unwrapped the wings, and opened the pizza box.

"I don't know what to say to that," Hammer finally said.

"Never mind," I said, around a mouthful of pizza. "We can talk about it when I get back. But there's something else to talk about, first."

"You mean Lisa?"

"Yeah."

"What's she want?"

"What makes you think she wants something?"

"Come on, Auggie," he said. "Everybody wants something. Did she tell you my daughter's name?"

"No."

"Or where she is?"

"No."

"But she'll sell you the information, right?"

"Yes." What I didn't tell him was that it was my idea, and she jumped at it.

"How much?"

"I don't know," I said. "We didn't get that far."

"You didn't make her an offer?"

"It's not my money, Hammer," I said. "I wouldn't know how much to offer her."

"Just make it life changing money."

"And how much is that?"

"I don't know," Hammer said. "You've seen her, where she lives, how she lives, how she looks. So you figure it out, and offer it to her."

"You sure you want to leave that up to me?"

"Just don't make it a million dollars," Hammer said. "Anythin' reasonable."

"So anything between a dollar fifty and a million?" I asked, kidding.

"Somethin' like that," he said, sourly.

"I'll give it some thought."

"You've got my number."

"I called that number earlier tonight. There was no answer."

"I'll keep it close, and on," he said. "When you get back maybe we can do somethin' to help your friend, Nikki."

"She's not my—" I started, but he hung up.

I ate my pizza and wings, rented a movie, and tried to figure out how much money was life changing.

CHAPTER 45

BY MORNING the only decision I had made was to have breakfast in the hotel, again. I was trying to decide whether or not to call Jack, my snack delivery man, for a ride, but the decision was made for me when I saw him in the breakfast room, sitting with a cup of coffee in front of him.

"'mornin'," I said. "Another delivery?"

"Nope, not today."

"Just came by for breakfast, then?" I asked. "Or just a cup of coffee."

"I thought we'd have breakfast together and then head over to the old chick with the great ass's house."

Well, I guessed that was as good a way as any to describe Lisa Martin.

"Okay, then," I said. "Let's eat."

She must have been waiting for us, because as we approached the front door, it opened and she stepped out.

"Glad you came early," she said. "He's still asleep."

Today she was wearing a robe, not those shorts that showed off her ass and legs. I could see Jack's disappointment on his face.

"So?" she asked. "How much?"

"Is this just for you, or for you and your daughter?" I asked.

"This is for me," she said. "Let her make her own deal. This is back child support, as far as I'm concerned."

"Hammer told me you didn't want anything from him back then," I told her.

"Sure, I said that," she said, "but I didn't mean it. I figured he'd send me somethin'. I didn't think he was gonna . . . you know, die. And now I know he didn't! So he owes me."

I still wondered, if I hadn't mentioned money first, if she'd be talking like this.

"So? Did you talk to Hammer?"

"I did."

"How much did he say to offer?"

"Twenty thousand."

She made a rude noise with her mouth, then opened her robe. She was naked underneath. She had big, solid breasts implants with dark nipples, and a pretty taut tummy for someone her age. Jack's eyes lit up.

"You see this?" she said. "I can use this to make twenty grand. I don't need twenty grand."

"What then?" I asked. "Fifty?"

She closed the robe, held it tightly, and thought a moment.

"A hundred."

"A hundred *grand*?" Jack asked, aghast.

"That's right," she said, "A hundred grand."

"It's a deal," I said.

"What?" Jack said.

"Relax, Jack," I sad. "Okay, Lisa, you've got your money. Now where's your daughter?"

"When I have my money in my hand," she said "you'll have my daughter's name and address in yours. Then you can make your deal with her."

"Look," I said, "I have to get back to Nashville—"

"I just met you," she said, "and you want me to trust you a hundred grand worth?"

I studied her. She was right. She didn't know me from Adam.

"Hold on," I said. "I'll make a call."

"I gotta go back inside," she said. "If he wakes up . . . look, I don't want him to know about this money. You go make your call, and then meet me at my job."

"You have a bank account?"

"What? Of course I got a bank account. It's got about fifty-six

Dollars in it."

"Tell me where it is. We'll meet there."

"What for?"

"You're going to give me your routing number and account number. I'm going to have Hammer direct deposit the money into your account."

"Today?"

"Yes."

"Jesus, that's great," she said. "I'll have to get rid of him--

she jerked her thumb toward the house, "—and then I can meet you at my bank."

"Okay, what bank?"

"Bank of the West."

"Is that a real bank?" I looked at Jack.

"Oh, yeah," Jack said.

"It better be," she said. "They got my fifty-six dollars."

"Get me the routing and account numbers."

"Where would that be?" she asked. "On my statement?"

"Just give me one of your blank checks."

"Okay," she said. "Hold on. My purse is just inside."

She opened the front door, reached in, rooted around a bit and came out with a check. She handed it to me.

"Okay," I said. "I'll call Hammer and have him make the transfer. Meet us at the bank in . . . two hours."

"Is that enough time?" she asked.

"I'll know by the time you get to your bank."

"Okay," she said, looking excited, "okay." She lowered her voice. "I'll see you in two hours."

"Right."

She went back inside. Jack and I walked to his truck.

"You're gonna give her a hundred thousand dollars?" he asked.

"I'm not," I said. "Hammer is."

"That's a lot of money."

"He wants to see his daughter."

"Yah, but," Jack said, "that's a lot of money."

"Just take me to this bank, Jack," I said. "I'll call Hammer."

We climbed into the truck and got going.

CHAPTER 46

"A HUNDRED GRAND?" Hammer asked.

"That's what she said."

"You couldn't bargain her down?" he asked.

"You told me to offer her life changing money," I said. "Do you want to see your daughter, or not?"

"Okay, okay," he said. "Tell me how to send the money."

"Go to your bank. They'll do it. Here are the numbers."

I read the numbers off the check while Jack careened down the street.

"You can go to the bank, can't you?" I asked. "I mean, they don't think you're dead, do they?"

"I'll take care of this," he said. "Just make sure you find my daughter. Are you sure this is Lisa Martin you're talkn' to?"

"I saw the tattoo."

"Oh."

"Yeah," I said. "It's her."

"Okay, then," Hammer said. "Stay in touch."

Jack stopped the truck and I looked out at the Bank of the West building.

"Say, Auggie, how much do you get paid for this job?"

"Just my fee," I said. "Why, do you want some money, too?"

He looked embarrassed.

"Well, you know, I'm drivin' you around when I'm supposed to be working'—"

"This was your idea Jack, not mine," I reminded him. "Look. Just go to work and I'll get a cab. I'm going to be here a while."

"Yeah, okay," he said. "I'll see you later."

"I won't need you, anymore," I said. "I'm going to get this done and then hop a plane back to Nashville. Thanks for all your help."

"Yeah, sure, you're welcome."

I got out of the truck and he drove away. I wondered what he had on his mind? The talk of a hundred thousand dollars seemed to affect him. Maybe he did want a piece, but even I wasn't getting any of it, so . . .

I went into the bank.

———

Nobody in the bank would discuss anything with me, because the account wasn't mine. It didn't matter that I was holding a blank check. So I had to wait for Lisa to show up. I was there twenty minutes—getting funny looks from the tellers and the bank manager—when she came rushing in, wearing tight jeans, a t-shirt and sandals. The only places she showed her age were the corners of her eyes and mouth, and a bit in her neck. Maybe she'd use some of the money to get those fixed.

"Is it here?" she asked.

"I don't know," I said. "I doubt it, since I only spoke to

Hammer about half an hour ago. But they won't tell me anything."

"Well, they'll tell me."

"Let's talk to the manager."

"Right."

———

It turned out the kind of transfer I was talking about was not as easy as flipping a switch. Even if the money was sent electronically from another bank, it wasn't immediately available. Lisa would have to wait at least 24 hours before she could touch it.

I didn't know if these were Federal banking rules, State rules, or simply rules of the Bank of the West.

Lisa and I sat in a couple of uncomfortable chairs, waiting for some news on the transaction. I tried Hammer, but he wasn't answering.

"What's goin' on?" she asked, as I put my phone away.

"I don't know," I said. "I'm sure he's working on it. Why don't you tell me about your daughter? How old was she when you told her Hammer was her father?"

"Forty."

"Forty? Why did you wait so long?"

"I was never gonna tell 'er," Lisa said, "but she badgered me about it."

"And she hadn't ever asked you about it before?"

"Well, sure, when she was a little girl," she said. "I told her stories—her father was a war hero, a truck driver, a busy man—"

"Not a musician?"

"No," she said, "I never told her that."

"Why not?"

She shrugged. "It didn't seem important. And, eventually, she stopped askin'. Until . . ."

"Until?"

Lisa took a deep breath, let it out slowly.

"We hadn't spoken for years," she said, "and then three years ago she came to me and asked me, point blank."

"Who her father was?"

"No." She turned her head and looked at me. "She asked me if Hammer Dylan was her father?"

CHAPTER 47

"WHAT THE—" I started. I stopped and tried again. "How did she know—"

"She didn't *know*," Lisa said, "not for sure. That's why she asked me."

"How did you react?"

"I was stunned," she admitted. "I never said his name, the whole time she was growing up."

"Then how did she come up with it?"

"I don't know," she said.

"So, what'd you tell her?"

"I lied," she said, "again, like I have her whole life."

"And?"

"And that was the last time she spoke to me."

"Lisa," I said, turning to face her, "do you actually know where your daughter is?"

"I know where she lives," she said. "But . . . I don't actually know if she's there now."

"Shit," I said, straightening.

"But I can tell you her name, her address, where she works . . ."

"The money was for putting me in touch with her," I said.

"Well," she said, "if she's home you'll be in touch with her."

"Okay," I said, "come on." I stood up.

"Where are we goin'?"

"To see if your daughter's home," I said. "If she is, we'll come back here and see about money. In fact, It should be here by then." I didn't know if that was true, but I had to know if Hammer's daughter was real before I let her have access to the money.

Lisa had a beat up 2000 Toyota Camry parked out front. She had to turn the key several times to finally get it started. I knew one thing she was going to do if—and when —she got the money.

"Her name's Bright Martin."

"Bright?"

"I was almost a hippie back then," she explained. "It's actually Bright Taylor Martin, but she goes by Taylor. She found Bright was not an advantage when applying for jobs."

"So Taylor Martin. What does she do for a living?"

"She doesn't have a career," Lisa said. "she just goes from job to job. But . . ."

"But what?"

"She sings."

"Ah."

Lisa drove us to a neighborhood that was several steps above her own. People kept their yards manicured and their houses painted.

"That one," she said. "The blue one."

"Looks quiet."

"She lives there alone."

"How long?" I asked.

"Ten or twelve years."

"Has she ever been married?"

"No."

"Why not?"

"Never found the right guy."

"I thought you said she was a lesbian?"

"Guy or girl."

"Did you ever marry?" I asked.

"No."

"And why not?"

"Because I'm always finding the wrong guys."

We got out of the car and went up the walk to the front door.

"Uh-oh," she said.

I saw what she meant. The mailbox was full. And there was a collection of newspapers on the front steps.

"Where could she be?" I asked.

"I don't know," Lisa said. "I know she wanted to pursue her music career. Where would she go for that?"

"There are a few places," I said. "L.A., Austin . . . and Nashville come to mind."

Lisa knocked on the door, hoping against hope that Bright would answer. Naturally, she didn't.

She turned to look at me. "Does this mean I don't get the money?"

"That depends," I said. "Do you have a key? There might be something inside that tells me where she went."

"Oh, noooo," she said, "we don't have that kind of relationship."

"Okay," I said, "I can get the door open, but you have to go in with me."

"Why?"

"In case I get caught," I said. "I'd want the owner's mother present."

"You think that'll make a difference?" she asked.

"Not really," I said.

She shrugged. "Okay, then."

"Let's go around back," I said, "just to be safe."

We circled the house and approached the back door. There was a fence around the yard, and the door was closed, so no one could see us.

I forced the door and we entered the kitchen. It was as neat and well-appointed as the outside of the house.

"Okay, we're in," Lisa said. "Now what?"

"Now we search."

"For what?"

"I don't know," I said, "but I will when I find it."

"So where do you start?" she asked.

"The most personal room," I said. "The bedroom."

"I was here once before," she said. "It's this way."

I followed her through the dining room and living room, down a hall to the bedroom.

I started by going through her drawers, opening and closing them quickly.

"Want me to leave?" Lisa asked.

"Why?"

"Because," she said, with a grin, "you're bound to come to her drawer of undies."

I ignored her and kept opening drawers. Yes, I did come to a drawer of frilly, silky undies. I made quick work of it and kept going.

Finished with the bedroom I went to the bathroom to

the medicine chest. I found Tylenol, Ibuprofen, diet pills, and Zoloft for depression.

"Lisa, was your daughter heavy?" I asked. "Fat?"

"At one time, she was a porker," she admitted, "but she lost a hundred pounds about six years ago."

"What about depression?"

"I don't know anythin' about that."

We left the bedroom and went to the living room. The first thing I saw was a shelf with framed photographs. I went over, had a look and froze.

"Lisa, who's this?" I showed her a photo.

"That's Bright," she said. "That's my daughter. She had lots of pictures taken when she lost the weight."

"And her hair?"

"Like you see there, blonde."

The last time I had seen the woman in the photo she wasn't blonde and her name wasn't Bright. She was a brunette who claimed to be 60, but she wasn't. She was a 43 year old I knew to be Nikki Rialto.

CHAPTER 48

I WASN'T sure what to do next.

Did Lisa not know that her daughter was a successful country singer using the name Nikki Rialto? Or was she hiding that fact from me? And what about Nikki? I'd known women to lie about their age before, but usually it was to appear younger, not older.

"Why are you still holdin' that?"

"She's a pretty girl." I set the framed photo down. "How old did you say she is?"

"Forty-three. She looks a little older for her age, but not much. All that weight loss, she needed some work on her skin, it didn't all turn out great."

I thought back to being in bed with a naked Bright/Nikki. Her skin did look a little . . . stretched. She had looked great for the 60 she claimed to be, but yeah, okay, a little worn for 43.

"Why don't we head back to the bank?"

"Why?" she asked. "You wanna cancel the transfer?"

"No, Lisa," I said, "I want to make sure it goes through."

"That's great!" she screamed, then throwing her arms

around me and kissing me. Then she kissed me again and I responded for a moment, but stepped back as her tongue wormed itself into my mouth.

"Sorry," she said, also stepping back and putting her hands in her back pockets. "I got excited. Um, what're you gonna do after the transfer?"

"Get my ass back to Nashville."

"You sure?" she asked. "It's a pretty cute ass."

I looked over at the photo of Bright/Nikki and said, "I'm sure."

When we got back to the bank the manager hadn't even missed us. We had to sit for another fifteen minutes before he called us over to his desk.

"All right," he said, "the transfer has gone through, but you won't have access to the money until tomorrow, Miss Martin."

"How do I know that?" she asked.

"Well, you could go on line and check your account—"

"I don't have a computer," she said. "I've got better things to do."

"Yes, well, all right," the man said, "come over to my desk and I'll show you on my computer."

Lisa looked at me and said, "Wait for me?"

"Sure." I needed a ride back to my hotel, anyway.

After he showed her that the money was technically in her account she came back to me and happily said, "Let's go get a drink."

"I don't think so," I said, "but you can drive me to my hotel."

"Yeah, okay," she said, "sure."

We went out to her Toyota. Once we were in the front seat she asked, "Are you sure about that drink? We could, ya know, celebrate."

"My hotel," I said.

"You're right," she said. "It'd be better to celebrate in your room."

She started the car and screeched away from the curb. It occurred to me that if I did celebrate her windfall with her in my room, it would mean I had sex with a mother and her daughter. Luckily, I'm not the kind of guy who has something like that on my bucket list.

CHAPTER 49

I HAD JUST GOTTEN off the plane in Nashville when my phone started ringing. It was as if somebody had been there waiting for me to show up. The first call was not a number I recognized.

"Hello?"

"Auggie, where are you?" It was Nikki.

"The airport. I just got back."

"I don't know if they're gonna give me another call," she said. "I need your help."

"You still in jail?"

"Where else would I be?"

"Good. I'll be right there. We need to talk."

I broke the connection, picked up my carry-on and started for the cab stand. Before I could get there it rang again. This time I knew the number.

"What?"

"What happened?" Hammer asked. "Did she get the money? Did you see my daughter?"

"Not exactly," I said. "But I was in her house."

"What?"

"Hammer, we need to meet."

"Now? Where?"

"No, not now," I said. "Right now I've got to go to jail."

"What?" He sounded totally confused, which was how I felt.

"I'll call you with a place," I said. "Be ready to meet me on short notice."

"Auggie—"

I hung up.

———

I asked for Detective Hollinger, and he took me in to see Nikki Rialto—who I now knew was Bright Martin, Hammer Dylan's daughter. Of course, the only way to know that for sure was with a DNA test.

Hollinger let me use an interview room with her. When I entered, she was seated at the table, still wearing the clothes she'd had on when then arrested her jeans and a t-shirt. Now that I knew who she was I could see the resemblance to her mother.

"Finally!" she said. "Where have you been?"

"Working," I said, sitting across from her. "Why didn't you ask for a lawyer?"

"I don't know any."

"They would've given you one."

"A public defender?" she asked. "I figured you'd know somebody. But I also thought maybe you could convince these people I didn't kill anybody."

"How would I know that?"

She looked surprised.

"You know me."

"Not well," I pointed out. "We're . . . acquaintances, at best."

"We're a little more than that, Auggie."

"Why? Because we had a one night stand?"

She frowned.

"Are you going to hold that against me?" she asked.

"Not at all," I said.

I didn't know if we were being recorded, so I didn't talk about my trip to Tulsa. I stood up.

"I'll get you a lawyer," I told her. "It'll be up to him to get you out on bail."

"Can he? Will he?"

"On a murder charge? We'll have to see."

"I didn't kill anyone."

"We have things to talk about," I said, "but it can wait until you get out."

"What things?" she asked.

"Bright things," I said, giving her a pointed look.

She sat back, as if I'd slapped her.

———

Hollinger was waiting for me in the hall.

"Got time to talk?" he asked.

"Why not?" I asked. "Your desk?"

"No, not here," he said. "Let's take a walk around the corner."

"Around the corner" meant a cop bar I knew he frequented. We walked there, but didn't start talking until we each had a pint of beer in our hands, and were seated at a table.

"What've you got on her?" I asked.

"That's for her lawyer to ask. Who are you gonna get her?"

"I don't know, yet."

"Well, you better do it quick. I've got to formally charge her and take her for arraignment."

"And then move her."

"Right."

"So what've you got for me?"

"Well, the guy in The Bluebird, I don't think that was Hammer Dylan."

"Why not? We got nothing back in prints."

I thought fast.

"He doesn't look like him."

"You know what Dylan would look like forty years later?" Hollinger asked.

"I talked with his agent, who doesn't think it was."

"That kid?"

"No, no, his real agent, the old man," I said. "The kid's grandfather. He was there that night and saw the guy."

"I thought he was out of the picture."

"Well, he's not dead," I said. "It made sense to me to talk to him."

Hollinger sighed.

"I guess it should have made sense to us, too, but to tell you the truth, we didn't even know he was there. The kid didn't mention it."

"Well," I lied, "take my word for it. He said it wasn't Hammer."

"That doesn't mean Rialto didn't think he was Hammer Dylan, and kill him."

"Why? What motive would she have?"

"We talked to a friend of hers, who said she told her that Hammer Dylan raped her when she was young."

Jesus, I thought, how many people did she tell that phony story to?

"I don't think she did it, Detective."

"Well, then," Hollinger said, "get me another suspect."

"What about the Axe Man?" I asked. "Are you still investigating both murders?"

"Yes, we are."

"As the work of one killer?"

"We haven't made that decision, yet," Hollinger said.

"If you figured Nikki for the first," I said, "would the second seem the work of a woman? I mean, with all the damage?"

"An angry woman, maybe," Hollinger said.

"What other kind of woman commits murder?" I asked.

"You better get her that lawyer quick," Hollinger advised.

"Right," I said. "Thanks."

———

We walked back to the police station together, and then while he went inside I took out my cell phone and remained outside. My use of criminal lawyers was negligible, but I knew one who had me serve papers from time to time. I called his office, got him on the phone after convincing his secretary he would want to talk to me.

"Auggie," Gerald Overmeyer said, "I don't have anything for you right now—"

"I think I have something for you, Gerald," I said. "It's murder."

CHAPTER 50

I WAITED out front for Overmeyer, and gave him the story. The whole story.

"So she's the forty-three year old daughter of music legend Hammer Dylan," he said "who claims to be a sixty year old woman who was raped by Hammer. Do I have that right?"

"In a nutshell."

"Which story do you believe?"

"Right now the daughter one," I said, "but I need to talk to her outside of the police station."

"Right," he said, "let me see what I can do."

Overmeyer was not one of the elite criminal lawyers in Nashville, but he was one of the busiest. He ran a one man shop and had been at it over twenty-years. He was a 54 year old man who kept himself in shape, and yet his suits always looked baggy. I had been introduced to him by Harley.

"How's Harley, by the way?" he asked.

"Hanging on," I said, "but wasting away."

"What a shame," he said, shaking his head. "Want me to call you?"

"I'm going to wait out here," I said. "I don't think they've got enough to charge hold her. I think you're going to come walking out with her."

"You've got a lot of faith in me."

"Maybe just no faith in the police's case."

━━

My faith in Overmeyer—or lack of faith in the police—was justified. In just under an hour the lawyer came out the front door with Nikki. They walked down the stairs, spoke briefly, and then shook hands. Overmeyer walked away, after waving to me. Nikki came over to me, stuck her hands in her pockets, and smiled at me.

"Thanks for that."

"You know what you're up against?"

She nodded. "As soon as they feel they have enough evidence, they'll come and get me."

"Are you going to run?"

"Where would I go?"

"Back to Tulsa," I asked, "Bright?"

"I thought maybe that wasn't a coincidence inside," she said. "How'd you find out?"

"I talked with your mother, went into your house," I said.

"Then you know I don't have a motive for murder."

"Not the motive you claimed to have," I said. "The rape."

"You think I wanna kill 'im because he was my father?"

"Maybe because he was your father, and you never knew," I said.

"Look, Auggie—"

"Let's go someplace we can talk," I suggested.

"Your place?" she asked. "I could use a shower."

"What's wrong with your place?"

"It's a hole," she said, "with no shower."

"Okay then," I said, "my place."

CHAPTER 51

SHE CAME out of the bathroom after her shower, wearing an X-large t-shirt I had at the bottom of a drawer. It didn't have a guitar on it. Instead it said I'D RATHER BE SINGING, and was dark red, so even though she was still damp, she wasn't exactly putting on a wet T-shirt show.

"Thanks for that," she said, running her fingers through her wet hair. "And this. Not one of your good ones, huh?"

"It was a gift," I said. "You want a beer?"

"Definitely."

I got two bottles from the frig, twisted off the caps and handed her one.

"Why are you lookin' at me like that, Auggie?" she asked, accepting it.

"Why would a forty-three year old woman claim to be sixty?" I asked. "It goes against everything I know about women."

"When I said I was sixty, how did you think I looked?"

"Great!"

"And now that you know I'm forty-three how do you think I look?"

I hesitated, searching for the right word. Hard? Worn? Weary? But still attractive. After all, it was in the genes.

"Never mind," she said. "I know I look older than I am, but I've had a hard life. I was fat for most of it, addicted to drugs for some of it. When I lost the weight my skin sagged, so I needed surgery for that. You know, to pull it taut? Neck, upper arms, thighs, that sort of thing." She was starting to talk faster and faster. "So when I came to Nashville to pursue my music I thought having people think I was older would help. I was trying to do the Bonnie Raitt thing. She's always looked great for her age, and sounded great. And it worked . . . for a while."

"Yeah, but . . . sixty?"

"I thought about fifty, but I thought maybe I already looked fifty. So I jumped it ten years. By the way, did you fuck my mother? You know, do that mother-daughter thing men are so fond of?"

"Hell, no!" I snapped. "That's not something that's been on my to-do list."

"Good, because I know she would've tried. She's never seen a man she didn't want to fuck."

I didn't point out that *we* had fucked the first night we met.

"Can we talk about something else?" I asked.

"Like what?"

"Murder."

"Sure," she said, "but . . . do you have something I can munch on?"

I went to the kitchen area, opened a cabinet, took out a fresh bag of potato chips, and tossed it to her.

"Thanks." She tore it open and started popping them into her mouth one at a time.

"Should I call you Bright, or Nikki?" I asked.

"I'm Nikki," she said. "That other one was my hippie mother's idea. I always hated it."

"Okay, Nikki," I said, "why did you decide to ask your mother who your father was after so many years?"

She chewed what was in her mouth, washed it down with a swig of beer. When she crossed her legs I could see she had nothing on beneath the shirt. I couldn't tell if it was a deliberate move or not. What I could see reminded me that she didn't wax.

"I heard a Hammer Dylan song on the radio," she said. "It reminded me of someone."

'Who?"

"Me." She put the bag of chips down and sat forward in her chair.

"I mean, I don't sound like him, but there was something . . . maybe the phrasing? I'm not sure, but in that moment I thought . . . wouldn't it be somethin' if Hammer Dylan was my dad?"

"So you asked your mother."

"I did." She nodded. "And I knew right away. I mean, she was stunned for a moment, but then she admitted it."

"That must have been . . . odd."

"It was," she said, "but it also convinced me that I should come to Nashville and really try."

"And not tell anyone that you're Hammer Dylan's daughter?" I
asked.

"Right."

"But telling people you're sixty, and that Hammer Dylan raped
you."

She bit her lip.

"You explained the age thing," I said. "What was the rape

talk all about?"

"I'm . . . not sure," she said. "I guess I thought a woman my age—and I mean sixty—needed to have some . . . drama, some . . . something tragic in her history."

"What've you done about line notes on your CDs?" I asked.

"I haven't had to deal with that, yet. No CDs."

"What?"

"Everything I've done has been on iTunes, so far."

"But you do intend to cut an album, at some point, right?"

"Well, yeah . . ."

"Have you told anybody else other than me that you were raped by Hammer? I mean, you must've told someone, because I sure as hell didn't tell the police."

"I have a couple of girls I thought were my friends," she said. "I guess one of them told the detective."

"And when you do your album . . ."

" . . . will I mention any of it? I don't know. Should I?"

"Well, the rape that never happened—"

"But it did," she said, cutting me off.

"What?"

"The rape did happen, Auggie," she said. "It just didn't happen to me. It happened to my mom."

CHAPTER 52

"SAY THAT AGAIN."

She sighed. "When I asked my mother if he was my father she said yes, and told me the story I told you, only it happened to her. Get it?"

"So it wasn't a forcible rape," I said. "She was underage."

"Hey, rape is rape, right?"

I didn't quite agree with that, but I kept it to myself for the moment.

"I still don't think you'd want to tell that story on your album, no matter who it happened to."

"He's dead, what's the difference?" She asked. "It would probably just add to his legend."

"That's not quite true," I said.

"What do you mean?"

"The reason I went to Tulsa in the first place was to look for you."

"But you knew where I was."

"Okay," I said, "I was looking for Hammer Dylan's daughter."

"Why?" She scrunched up her face. "How'd you even know he had a daughter?"

"Because," I said, "he hired me to find her—you."

She was taken aback by that statement.

"What? I thought—he's alive?"

"His agent hired me to find that out," I said. "Then Hammer himself came to me, asked me to find you."

"Are you sure it's him?"

"Actually, no," I said. "I think the only person who's going to be able to tell me that is his original agent. I was hired by the grandson, who's running the agency, now."

"Have you told the police he's alive?" she asked.

"No."

"That would get me off the hook, you know."

"Not exactly," I said. "There's still a dead man—two dead men, actually."

"Two?"

"The Axe Man," I said.

"Is that—are the two connected?"

"The police think so."

"Why would I kill a guy who owns a music store?" she asked.

"That's what they're trying to find out," I said. "Motive."

"Well, I don't have one."

She went back to the bathroom, came out dressed in the same clothes as before. She could have kept the t-shirt, but I didn't say that.

"When can I meet him?" she asked.

"You want to see him?"

"Well, sure," she said. "He's my dad."

Did I want to put Nikki in a room with Hammer? There were two things I still wasn't sure of. 1, if Nikki killed the guy at the Bluebird, thinking he was Hammer, and two, if the man presenting himself to me as Hammer Dylan actually was.

It was probably time to make a few phone calls.

———

Nikki left me a phone number where I could reach her after I spoke to Hammer about seeing her.

"But," she added, "I'd appreciate it if you'd make sure it's him before we do that."

"I plan to," I assured her.

After she left I grabbed my cell and called Hammer.

"She wants to see you."

"Where and when?"

"I'll pick you up tomorrow morning and we'll talk about it," I said. "Now you tell me where and when?"

He did.

———

Next I called Carter Three.

"Is he there, Nancy?" I asked, when she answered.

"Hey, Auggie, he's on another line, right now—"

"Tell him I found him," I said. "I found Hammer."

"Hold on!" she said, excitedly. "I'll get him."

It only took a few seconds for Carter to come on and blurt, "You found him, Auggie?"

"I think so."

"Whataya mean you think so?" he asked, suddenly losing some of his polish.

"Well, he says he's Hammer Dylan," I said. "I need somebody to confirm it for me."

"What about fingerprints? DNA?"

"He'd have to be in the system," I said.

"So what are we gonna do?"

"I want to talk to your grandfather," I said.

"Today? He's probably—"

"Let's do it tomorrow, then," I suggested.

"Where?"

"Your grandfather's house."

"I don't know if they'll let me in," Carter admitted.

"Say the secret word," I advised, and broke the connection.

My next call was to Carter Senior's house. Evangeline answered the phone.

"Vangie, it's Auggie Velez."

She was quiet.

"I'm sorry, do I call you Vangie, Evangeline, or Mrs.—"

"What do you want, Mr. Velez?" she asked, coolly.

"I need to speak with your father-in-law—"

"He's resting, right now."

"—tomorrow," I finished. "When would be a good time."

"What's it about?" she asked.

"Hammer Dylan."

She was quiet, then she said, "Come by at noon," and hung up.

I called Hammer again and told him I would pick him up at 11:30 tomorrow morning.

"I can come to where you're staying," I said.

"The street corner will do," he said, sticking to the original plan.

I was tired of getting hung up on, so I stopped making calls.

But my phone wasn't done. It chirped at me as I was pouring myself a cup of coffee from my Mister C. It was

Jesse Fogarty. Jesus, I'd forgotten I had him sitting on the post office box in Anthem.

"Jesse, how you doing?" I asked, trying to sound casual.

"How would you be doin' if you were sleepin' in your car and peeing into a bottle?" he asked.

"That's what I like to hear," I said, "commitment to the job."

"Yeah. You still wanna know who's hittin' that P.O. box?"

"I do."

"Big guy, and I mean height and belly. Long beard, jeans and a plaid shirt, looks like he should be with Willie, Waylon and the boys."

"Gotcha," I said. "You're done, Jesse."

"That's it? I can go someplace and take a decent crap?"

"Go home, shower, crap, whatever. I'll send you a check."

"Let's meet in a bar somewhere and you can give me cash," he said. "Deal?"

"Deal, but it'll be a few days."

"No problem. Harley says I can trust you."

Guess what?

He hung up on me.

CHAPTER 53

I PICKED Hammer up the next morning at the agreed upon time on the corner of Broadway and 8th. He was dressed the same way Jesse had seen him at the p.o. box in Anthem.

"You eat breakfast?" I asked.

"Hours ago."

"Early riser, huh?"

"I don't sleep much," he admitted. "You?"

I had slept good, risen early and eaten at the Back Alley.

"I'm good," I said.

"Cool. Now tell me about my daughter."

"Lisa named her 'Bright.'"

"Bright Martin?"

"Yup."

He shook his head and chuckled. "She always was a hippie, that chick. She still look good?"

"She looks great," I said. "Hot looking sixty year old."

"Well," Hammer said," she did look older than she was when I knew 'er, so now she looks younger than she is. Figures."

"How much?" I asked.

"How much what?"

"How much older did she look back then?"

"I know what you're gettin' at," he said, looking at me. "She was eighteen goin' on twenty-five."

"Not according to Nikki."

"Nikki? Who's Nikki?"

"Oh, didn't I mention? Bright changed her name to Nikki."

"Nikki, that's a lot better. Wait . . . are you tellin' me Nikki Rialto—"

"—is your daughter. And she was arrested for killing you. And the way to get her off the hook is for you to be alive."

"Yeah."

"But that's for later," I said. "Nikki told me you raped her mother."

"After she told you I raped *her*? No wonder I didn't remember her. Wait! How old is she?"

"Never mind," I said. "How old was Lisa when you had sex with her?"

"I told you I never raped anybody, Auggie, and I meant it. She said she was eighteen. She looked twenty-five. I'm not lyin' about that."

"Uh-huh." The other thing he could have been lying about was being Hammer Dylan in the first place. The word could've gotten around that I was asking about him, and he decided to cash in. Or it really was him. I was hoping Carter Senior would be able to tell me.

I could've done this at the start, but everything started to happen, he hit me with the daughter stuff, and I wasn't ready to put him together with Carter Three, yet. And then the murders . . .

Maybe Harley would've done it different, but I was still learning this P.I. stuff. He'd taught me all he could before the cancer took him out of the game. Now I was on my own, making my own decisions and living with them, right or wrong.

If today solved the Hammer Dylan question, then tomorrow could solve the daughter question. Then all that would be left were the murders, and that was up to the cops.

"Where are we goin'?" Hammer asked.

"To get some answers."

I pulled into the driveway of Carter Senior's house, stopped the car and looked at Hammer. He kept staring ahead.

"You're not asking me who lives here," I said

"So?"

"That means you already know."

"So, I've been here before."

"Did Carter Senior live here forty years ago?" I asked. "Or have you been here recently?"

"Why don't we just go inside and get this over-with," he suggested.

"Sure," I said, "why not?"

We walked up to the front door and rang the bell. Evangeline opened the door, took one look at him, and said, "No, you're not supposed to be here."

"Tell him that," Hammer said, pointing to me.

CHAPTER 54

I FINALLY CONVINCED Vangie that she should let us in.

"I'm sure your father-in-law is expecting us."

"He is," she admitted. "I told him you were coming—and I mean, just you."

"Yeah, well," I said, as we entered the foyer, "Carter's coming, too."

"*My* Carter?"

"How many are there?" I asked. "Carter One and Carter Three, right? And One is already here, so yeah, your Carter."

"Don't get snotty with me, Mr. Velez," she snapped. "And why is Carter coming? He hasn't been here in months."

"Well," I said, "he did hire me to find Hammer. And judging by the look on your face, I've done that."

She looked at Hammer, and then quickly turned away.

"He's waiting," she said.

She led the way through the house and out the back to the patio where I'd first met him. I'd seen him once since then, at The Bluebird, and he looked as if he had aged since then. He was sitting under an umbrella to keep the sun off. His skin was pale and almost looked translucent. He was staring off into the distance and as we approached he looked up at us. At that point the doorbell rang.

"That's probably Carter," Vangie said. "I suppose I should let him in, too."

She went back into the house.

"The kid's here?" Carter Senior asked, suddenly becoming animated.

"Yeah, he's here," I said. "It's time for all of us to get together."

"What for?" Old Man Bannister asked.

"To introduce Carter to Hammer," I said.

Bannister looked at Hammer.

"What're you doin' here?" he asked him.

"He brought me," Hammer said. "I didn't know we were comin' here."

"You've been here before," I said.

"So what?"

"Then as we got closer, you knew where we were going, and you didn't stop me."

"What was I supposed to do, grab the wheel?"

"You could've said something."

"Why?" he asked. "I figured we were gonna end up here sooner or later."

"So you've known all these years that he wasn't dead," I said to Bannister the Original.

"What?"

Carter Three came walking out of the house with his mother.

"You knew?" he asked his grandfather.

"Now, look--" Bannister started.

"Why didn't you ever tell me?" Carter went on. "When

I told you I wanted to open the agency and look for him, why didn't you tell me he was alive? Instead, I had to hire Auggie to find out."

"Don't yell at your grandfather!" Vangie snapped. "Hammer's his friend."

"I'm his family."

"What kind of family never comes around?" she demanded.

"What kind of mother doesn't help her son?" he snapped back. "*You* knew he was alive, too, didn't you?"

"Yes, I knew, but I was under no obligation to tell you."

"It would've saved a lot of time," Carter said, "and money." I didn't say anything about the last part, even though he hadn't paid me anything. In the group, Hammer was my only paying client. And by now, I knew that he actually was Hammer Dylan.

"Well," I said, aloud, "my work is done here."

They all turned and looked at me.

"Whataya mean?" Hammer asked.

"Carter hired me to find out if you were dead or alive, and if alive, find you and put the two of you together." I pointed. "Carter Three? This is Hammer Dylan. Hammer? This is your agent."

"That's my agent," Hammer said, pointing at Carter Senior.

I waved my hand. "That's for all of you to figure out. But you're still alive, and the word is going to get out. Deal with it."

"Hey wait!" Hammer said, as I started into the house. He trotted alongside me on the way to the front door. "What about my daughter? You gotta get me together with her."

We stopped at the front door.

"I'm still going to do that," I said. "I'll talk to her, call you and set it up. Now you better get back out there before they tear each other apart."

I could hear them yelling at each other as I went out the front door.

CHAPTER 55

I WAS WISHING I hadn't gotten involved with the whole Hammer Dylan thing. There was a father-in-law/daughter-in-law battle going on, a mother/son dispute, a grandfather/grandson conflict, and a dead man walking. Why did I need to be involved with any of that? It looked like I was never going to be paid by the Bannister Agency, and I'd already been paid by Hammer. So all I needed to do was put him together with Nikki, and walk away—and walking was sounding more and more like a viable option.

I waited until I got back home to call Nikki.

"Can't we do this today?" she asked.

"Well, *you* can," I said, "if you want to go to his agent's house and be a referee."

"That doesn't sound doable," she admitted. "So what are you doin' about my case?"

"What case?"

"If you remember, I was arrested for murder?"

"It doesn't seem to me they have much evidence against you," I said, "and you do have a lawyer."

"Yeah, but I need a good private eye to find out who the murderer is."

"The cops are investigating."

"Okay, let's put it this way," she said. "I need somebody to prove I'm not the murderer."

"I can't work on an active police case, Nikki," I said. "Not without risking my license."

"Well, what if you were workin' for my lawyer? Don't they need investigators?"

"I can't ask your lawyer to hire me," I said. "And yes, they usually do use investigators."

"Then I'll ask him to hire you."

"If he calls, I'll talk to him," I promised.

"Haven't you worked with him before?"

"Actually, yes, but only to serve summonses on people."

'Well, I'm supposed to talk to him today," she said. "When do I get to meet Hammer?"

"Tomorrow," I said.

"Where?"

"Here, my place," I said. "I'll have him here at noon."

She took a deep breath, let it out and said, "I'll be there."

"See you then," I said, and broke the connection.

Next I called Detective Hollinger. I thought I owed it to him.

"He's what?" he exclaimed.

"Alive," I said, "Hammer Dylan is alive."

"Where's he been all these years?"

I could have said "Anthem, Tennessee," but although it seemed likely, I wasn't sure. I intended to get that out of him the next day, before Nikki showed up.

"You'll have to ask him that."

"Well, where is he now?"

"He's at his agent's house," I said, and gave him the address.

"Are you sure about this?" he asked.

"Positive," I said. "His agent confirmed it."

"So the dead guy at The Bluebird wasn't Dylan," he said, "and we still don't know who he was."

"I guess that means Nikki didn't kill Hammer Dylan."

"Nice try," Hollinger said, "but that doesn't mean she didn't kill the dead guy, thinking he was Hammer Dylan. Or that she didn't kill your Axe Man."

"So you're still on her, huh?"

"I told you," he said. "Find me somebody else. Thanks for the word on Dylan, we'll go and check that out. Maybe he killed the Axe Man."

I didn't comment on that. I just told him he was welcome, and hung up. Hammer was keeping something from me, I felt sure of that, but was it murder? And why would he have wanted to kill Hoyt Bennett, who he had known for years and backed in his store?

I had been asked by two clients to find somebody, which I had done. Was I now going to end up working two murders? If Nikki did manage to get Gerald Overmeyer to hire me to work the case, did I want to? Harley Rayborn had always told me the one kind of case a P.I didn't want to work was a murder.

"If your client turns out to be guilty, you don't get paid," he'd told me. Which was a good point.

The main reason for not working a murder is that they're usually active police cases. Nikki was right, I'd be able to work it if I represented her attorney.

I had started to spread out my meal choices of late, which was why I was in the Rock Bottom Brewery instead of the Back Alley when my cell sounded. It was Overmeyer.

"'evenin', Gerald."

"Your girl wants you on this," he said, without preamble.

"She's not my girl," I said.

"Your friend, then," he corrected. "I told her I had my own man, but she wants you. What do you say?"

"Is she paying you?"

"We worked that out."

"Then you're paying me?"

"Yes."

"Okay, then."

"Can you come by my office tomorrow so we can work out a strategy?" he asked.

"Sure."

"Nine a.m.?"

"Let's make it ten," I said. "And I have to be back at my place by noon."

"Shouldn't be a problem."

"Then I'll see you tomorrow," I said, and broke the connection as the waitress brought me my plate. "Another pint, please." I said.

CHAPTER 56

THE STRATEGY MEETING at Overmeyer's office didn't take long. Basically, he was asking me for the same thing Hollinger had been asking for—another suspect.

When I got back to my place Nikki was waiting in front of the Boogie. She had a bag. She was a half hour early.

"I brought coffee," she said.

"How many?"

"Three."

"Good."

We went upstairs.

"He'll be here at noon," I told her, as she handed me a cup of coffee.

"That's good," she said. "Gives me a chance to catch my breath."

She walked to the sofa and sat, drank her coffee.

"I just came from Overmeyer's office," I told her. "I'm on the job."

"What's your first step?"

"My first step," I said slowly, "is to have you convince me that you're innocent."

"But I am!"

"I know you've told me and the police that," I said. "Did you convince them?"

"Well, no . . ."

"So convince me."

———

Nikki tried for an hour, but most of what she came up with was along the lines of, "I didn't do it, damn it!"

I checked my watch, saw that it was 12:30. Hammer was a half hour late.

"Where is he?" she asked, noticing me to glance at my wrist.

"One thing you should know about Hammer Dylan," I said, "is that he runs on his own clock."

"So does my mother, and so do I," she said. "I guess that means we deserve each other."

I thought about making a "Hammertime" comment, but didn't think she was in the mood for humor. No chance she'd come back at me with "Can't touch this!"

Well, since she had been lying about her age when we slept together, she was right. They all did deserve each other.

At one o'clock she said, "He's not comin', is he?"

"He's Hammer Dylan," I said. "He's a sonofabitch, but that's no excuse, I know."

She walked to the window and looked down at the street, but she wasn't looking for him.

"I guess I've got bigger problems than findin' my father," she said.

"Like beating a murder rap," I said. "You're gonna have to work closely with Overmeyer."

"And you?"

"I'll do what I can," I said, "but you have to help me."

She turned and looked at me.

"What do you wanna know?"

"Forget about Hammer for now," I said. "Sit down and let's start from the beginning."

"The very beginning?" Nikki asked, moving to the sofa and sitting.

"No," I said. "Nashville."

"I came to Nashville a few years back for two reasons," she said. "To advance my career, and to find my father. It happened for my career, first."

"Why pretend to be sixty years old?"

"That was for you," she said. "If you've read anythin' about me, you noticed that I don't ever give my age. I let people wonder."

"I didn't know that," I admitted.

"When I saw the flier you guys put out for the Hammer Dylan tribute, I had to come."

"What made you think Hammer was still alive?"

"No body," she said. "It's not an Elvis thing. With Elvis they had a body, and people still think he's alive. There was never a Hammer Dylan body. And like you said, he's got his own clock."

"Did you discuss this with your mother?"

"Only after I found out for sure he was my dad," she said. "She told me to forget him, because he was dead—if not for real, then to us."

"But you didn't buy it."

"No. My mama and me, we hardly ever see eye-to-eye on anythin'."

"So all she had to do was tell you to forget it, and don't go to Nashville."

"And I was on the next bus."

"What were you hoping for when you came to The Bluebird that night?"

"I was hopin' I'd see him, maybe hidin' in the back."

"And did you see the man you're accused of killing, back there?" I asked.

"I did."

"Did you ever think he might be Hammer?"

"Just for a second," she said, "but I knew from my mama that Hammer had been a big man. I thought maybe he might've been sick, lost a lot of weight, but when I got a closer look at the man, I decided it wasn't him."

"How much of a closer look did you get?"

"Not close enough to stab him," she said. "I swear."

I was starting to believe her.

"When are you seeing Overmeyer again?" I asked.

"Four this afternoon, at his office."

I checked my watch again. Hammer *could* still show up.

"What do you wanna do until then?" I asked her.

Nikki gave me a look, a slow smile and asked, "Ya'll wanna fuck?"

CHAPTER 57

AFTER NIKKI LEFT for her meeting with Overmeyer—and yes, we did fuck, for a good long while—I tried calling the number I had for Hammer. Not only did he not answer, but the phone didn't even ring. I got a message saying that number was "unavailable."

Damn it, Hammer had done a disappearing act. But maybe all I had to do was call or go see his agent—and I didn't mean the kid Carter Bannister, but the old man.

On the other hand, I had a feeling I may know somebody else who could put me in touch with Hammer Dylan.

Having the scent of Nikki on me the rest of the day would've been distracting, so I took a quick shower, put on a Lita Ford t-shirt and headed out.

—————

Miss Avery greeted me at Harley's door.

"It's been a bad day, Mr. Velez."

"I won't be here long," I said. "I swear."

"Are you sneaking him a hot dog, or a beer?"

"Nothin'," I said. "Not today. I swear."

"All right," she said. "I was just making him a cup of tea. You can take it in to him."

"Okay, thanks."

When Harley saw me walk in with a tea cup he growled, "That better have beer in it."

"Not today, Harley," I said. "Miss Avery frisked me good."

"Damn," he said. "Tea?"

"Tea."

I set it down by the bed. He looked more drawn and pale than I'd ever seen him before, with bags under his pain-filled eyes. He was in his 70s, but he looked 20 years older.

He struggled to sit up, but when I tried to help him with his pillows he snapped, "I got it!"

"Sorry."

"No," he said, "I'm sorry. I'm just tired of bein' treated like glass. And yeah, yeah, I know, I got shattered glass inside me. I can feel it when I breathe. What brings ya here today?"

"Hammer Dylan."

"Still workin' on that?" he asked.

"Tell me the truth, Harley," I said. "You know 'im, don't you?"

"Well . . ."

"Come on, you're both about the same age, you were both here in Nashville at the same time all those years ago. That's really how I ended up involved isn't it?"

"Okay, yeah, I've known Hammer a long time."

"And did you know he was alive?"

"Not in the beginning," Harley said, "but after about a dozen years or so he showed up on my doorstep needin' help. We been in touch since then. So when he needed a private eye this time, and I couldn't help 'im."

"So where is he?"

"What?" Harley asked. "I thought you were workin' for him."

"So did I," I said. "He was supposed to come by my place at noon today and meet his daughter. He never showed."

"Did you call him?"

"The number he gave me is no longer in service," I said. "Do you have one?"

"Yeah," Harley said, "I got a number he gave me a long time ago, in case I needed 'im. Lemme have my cell, it's on the dresser."

I grabbed Harley's cell, which was one of those old folding kind. He only used it to make and get calls, didn't care about all the other "smart" options cell phones have, these days.

"Here ya go."

He winced as he tried to straighten up, took the phone from me and dialed a number. He listened, and then closed his phone.

"Same thing," he said. "No longer in service. I don't like this."

"I've got one option left," I said. "I'll go out and see Carter Bannister."

"The kid?"

"No," I said, "the original."

"Well," he said, settling back against his pillows again, "lemme know what happens."

"I will," I said. "Drink that tea."

"Yuck."

I drove to Carter Bannister the Original's house, parked my car in the driveway, behind a Porsche 011 and rang the front doorbell. No answer. I rang again with the same result.

With the Porsche in the driveway I assumed somebody was home. Either they were in the back by the pool and couldn't hear the bell, or were choosing not to answer.

I decided to check and see which one was the truth.

I left the front porch and walked around the side of the house, until I reached the gate leading to the pool area. It had a lock, but it wasn't fastened. In fact, the heavy iron gate was ajar.

I swung it open and entered, stepped up onto the tile surrounding the sunken pool. The chairs were pushed back from the tables, as if people had risen in a hurry. One was even lying on its back, which didn't make me feel good. Then I looked in the pool, and spotted a patch of fading, floating red.

I moved closer to the edge, and saw deeper red on the tiles, which had leaked into the water. I didn't have to do a T.V. thing, touch it with my fingers and smell it. I didn't even have to squat down to know that it was blood.

Fuck.

I turned and looked at the house. The French doors were wide open. It would be nothing for me to go inside and have a look around, but I was afraid of what I'd find. The smart thing would be to call the police and let them come and investigate.

So why did I go inside?

CHAPTER 58

I WENT through the open doors and looked around. There was no blood on the doors, or on the tile in front of it. I went to where the tile turned to carpet, still no blood. If there had been a body by the pool, they didn't drag it into the house.

"Hello? Anybody here?"

My voice seemed to echo, and the house felt very empty.

"Damnit!" I swore.

I was mad at myself for even entering the house, but since I was already going to have to explain it to the police, I figured I might as well finish looking around. Harley taught me that the cops have one way, and one way only, of searching a crime scene. It was up to him and me to find what they didn't.

I searched the first floor, found it void not only of people and blood stains, but anything helpful. I spent more time in Evangeline's home office, went through her French desk, studied the floor, but came up with nothing.

I left Vangie's office, went upstairs. checked all the bedrooms and bathrooms up there, and found nothing. I was relieved not to find any bodies, but frustrated not to find anything. But blood on the pool tiles, and in the water was reason enough to call the police, so I went back downstairs, out by the pool, took out my cell and dialed 9-1-1. I then went out in front of the house to wait.

Because Carter Bannister was rich—and, of course, the blood—the uniforms came, took one look at the pool area, and called for their supervisor, and detectives.

"Mr. Velez?"

The uniforms had allowed me to snag one of the pool chairs, take it off to the side and sit. As an obviously experienced detective in a wrinkled suit came over and called my name, I stood up.

He was holding my P.I. license, which the first cops on the scene had taken from me.

"Here ya go," the detective said, handing it back to me. "You got much experience at P.I. work?"

"A few years on my own," I said, "but I interned with Harley Rayborn for a lot of years,"

"I know Rayborn," he said. "I heard he's pretty sick."

"Cancer," I said, "but he's fightin' it."

"Good to hear," the man said. "I hope he makes it. Listen, I'm Detective Sheldrake. I need you to tell me what happened here."

I told him I was working for the Bannister Agency, came out to talk to Bannister Senior, and found an empty house and blood in the pool.

"That's it?" he asked.

"That's it."

"Did you go into the house?"

"I did." I had decided to be truthful. "I went lookin' for him or his daughter-in-law, Evangeline. When I realized the house was empty, and the doors unlocked, I came outside and called you guys."

"And that's it?" Sheldrake asked.

"What more could there be?"

"What was bringing you out here?"

"I told you, the agency is my client."

"And what's the case?"

I decided to play it straight. After all, I had nothing to hide.

"They hired me to find Hammer Dylan."

"What?" he said. "You mean . . . *the* Hammer Dylan?"

"That's the one."

"I thought he was dead."

"So did a lot of people," I said. "Dead like Elvis."

"Ah. So, did you find him?"

"I have no idea where he is," I said, truthfully. I wasn't giving him all of it. Not yet, anyway.

"I see. Did you leave your number with the officers?"

"I did."

"Well then, you can go," he said. "We'll look around here, and if we need anything else, we'll call you."

"And would you let me know what you find?" I asked. "If anything? I mean, I'd like to have somebody to bill for my time."

"We'll be in touch, Mr. Velez."

"Thanks."

I started to walk away.

"Oh," he called out, and I turned, "give Harley my best, will you?"

"Sure."

CHAPTER 59

I LEFT Bannister the Original's house and drove to Bannister the Third's office. It was late, but they were there. Nancy looked up from her desk when I walked in.

"Well, look who's here," she said, pleasantly. "No bagels?"

"Not this time. Sorry."

"I thought you were done with us?"

"I am," I said, "I did my job. By the way, my bill is still outstanding."

"Would you believe the check's in the mail?"

"Is he in?"

"I'll check." She picked up her phone. "What's it about?"

"Hammer."

She pressed a button and said, "Auggie's here. He says it's about Hammer." She hung up. "Go on in."

I went into Carter's office, found him sitting in shirt-sleeves behind his desk. There was a sheen of perspiration on his face, even though the air-conditioning was on.

"Where is he?" he asked, anxiously.

"That's what I'm here to ask you," I said. "He was supposed to be at my place at noon today, to meet his daughter. The last time I saw him he was with you and your family."

"Family." He almost spat the word. "They're not my family."

"They allowed you to start the agency up again."

"Allowed, yes," he said, "but they offer no help. Hammer's a perfect example."

"All right, well, what happened after I left yesterday?" I asked.

"We blew up," Bannister said, "like we always do. I got out of there, after Hammer agreed to meet me here later."

"And did he?"

"No."

"Have you talked to your grandfather or mother since then?"

"No."

"Did you try to call them?"

"I don't want to talk to them!" he said. "I just want to talk with Hammer."

"Carter," I said, "I just came from the house. Nobody's there, and there was blood in the pool."

"What?"

"I called the police, they're interested now," I went on. "They're gonna want to talk to you."

"About what?"

"To find out what you know."

"I don't know anything," he insisted. "I left the three of them at the house."

"Were they arguing?" I asked.

"Only with me," he said, sternly.

"Well, after you left something happened," I said. "Either yesterday, or sometime today."

He stared at me, then his features softened.

"Is somebody dead?"

"I don't know."

"Was there enough blood for that?"

"It would depend," I said. "If somebody had been shot or stabbed, and then moved right away, there'd be the small amount of blood I saw."

"How small?"

"Bigger than you'd get from a paper cut," I said. "It's gonna be up to the cops to find out."

"When will they come for me?" he asked.

"I came here from there," I said. "It won't be long."

"Then I better go home, so they can find me," he said. "I'll close up the office."

"Okay," I said. "I'm heading home, too."

"Thanks, Auggie. If you hear from the cops before I do, will you let me know what they find out?"

"I will."

I left his office.

"What's goin' on, Auggie?" Nancy asked.

"I'll let Carter tell you," I said. "I've got to get home, in case Hammer's trying to find me there."

"But what—"

"Sorry."

I left the office and headed home.

My thinking was that maybe his phone wasn't working. In that case, Hammer might have gone to my place to find me.

I stopped off and got enough chicken for two people, then went straight to my place to wait.

He wasn't out front, so I went upstairs. I didn't expect to find him there, and I was right. I tried his phone again, got the same message.

Something had happened at the Bannister house. Maybe it had happened to Hammer, or maybe he was on the run. Or maybe it had happened to the old man, or Vangie. In either case, Hammer could be in hiding.

I set the phone down on the coffee table, opened the box of chicken and started to eat. I was on my second piece when the downstairs buzzer sounded. I went to the door.

"Who is it?"

"Nikki. Have you heard from him?"

"No, but—"

"Can I come up?"

"Are you hungry?"

"Starved," she said. "And I have a six-pack."

"Then you better come up."

I buzzed her in.

CHAPTER 60

WE SAT TOGETHER on the sofa and ate, while I told her what had been happening.

"Jesus," she said, "and you still haven't heard from Hammer?"

"Not a peep," I said. "Nobody has. But the police are gonna be looking for him, now."

"At least my daddy and I have somethin' in common," she said, biting into a chicken leg. "The cops are after us."

"Well, they'll want him for questioning," I said. "Your problem's a little different."

"Yeah," she said, "murder of a man I didn't even know."

"How did your meeting with Overmeyer go?"

"Fine," she said. "I don't have any witnesses that say I didn't kill the man."

"But the police don't have any who can say you did."

"Right," she said. "It's a stand-off, but they're not gonna accept that."

"So they'll keep investigating."

"Yes. You gonna eat those fries?"

"No, they're all yours."

We finished eating and I cleaned up—which means I tossed everything into the garbage, except a few spare pieces of chicken, which went into my fridge. Then we popped the caps off the last of her six-pack and sat back on the sofa.

"Are you gonna wanna fuck?" she asked, slurring her words slightly. "If so I better not finish this one. It's gonna put me to sleep."

"No," I said, "fucking wasn't on my schedule tonight You can go home and go to sleep."

"Oh," she said, leaning her head back against the sofa cushion, "I thought I'd just sleep right here."

"Nikki," I said, "as much as I like fucking, I'm not really comfortable sharing my bed—"

"No, no," she said, "that's okay. I meant . . ." she slapped her hand down on the cushion next to her, " . . . right here."

I managed to get the beer bottle out of her hand before she dropped it. There was only a slug or two left, as she drifted off on the sofa.

I got a pillow and blanket, and managed to make her comfortable without waking her up. Then I went and sat on my bed, finishing my own bottle. Somewhere along the line, I set the bottle down on the floor and fell asleep myself . . .

———

When I woke in the morning Nikki was still asleep on the sofa. I slipped out and came back with half dozen bagels and 4 containers of coffee.

I buttered the bagels, put them on a plate, then took the plate to the coffee table and set them down with the open containers of java. The smell did their work, and her eyes fluttered.

"Huh? Wha—"

"Good-morning," I greeted, chewing on my own sesame bagel.

"Is it mornin'?" she asked, sitting up. She removed the blanket, swung her feet to the floor and reached for one of the coffees.

"It is."

She picked up a blueberry bagel and bit into it.

"You're a very carin' man, you know," she said. "Pillow, blanket, breakfast . . . a girl might think you didn't want to get rid of her."

"I don't," I said. "I mean, I don't want you to move in, but I'm not trying to get rid of you—"

She cut me off by laughing.

"Keep calm, Auggie," she said. "I'm not lookin' to move in. I've got my own place, I just wanted to sleep here in case the cops came lookin' for me last night."

"I get it."

"Can I take a shower before I leave?"

"Sure."

"And borrow a clean t-shirt?"

I had a mouthful of bagel and coffee, so I waved and nodded.

"Thanks."

She took her coffee and bagel into the bathroom with her, and I heard the shower go on.

I switched over to the sofa, started on my second bagel and coffee. She came out wrapped in a towel, drying her hair with another one. Nikki Rialto may have been over some rough road in her life, but there was something sexy about her, made even sexier now that she was wrapped in a wet towel.

"Can I pick a shirt?" she asked.

"Help yourself."

She knew what drawer they were in, so went to it and chose one with one hand while still drying her hair with the other. With both hands occupied, the towel she was wrapped in fell to the floor.

"Oops," she said, but made no effort to catch it.

"Clapton okay?" she asked.

"Fine."

She turned so I could see her nipples and pubic patch, then picked up the towel and simply held it in front of her. With the shirt and two towels, she went back to the bathroom, giving me a view for a few steps of her pert butt. Unlike her mother, there was no tattoo there—but I could see the family resemblance.

The next time she came out she was wearing the Clapton t-shirt, her jeans and, presumably, the same underwear. Her feet were bare, her shoes in front of the sofa.

"That feels better," she said. "Is that other coffee for me?"

"Yep," I said, "two each. And more bagels."

"Another bagel and I'll get fat," she said, sitting next to me and reaching for her shoes. Once she had them on she grabbed the other coffee and started drinking. Her hair was still wet, which didn't seem to bother her.

My phone sounded then, just a normal ring, no fancy ring tone.

"Hello?"

"Mr. Velez? This is Detective Sheldrake. We met at Carter Bannister's house?"

"I remember," I said. "Have you found 'em? Carter or Vangie?"

"No, not yet," Sheldrake said. "I was wondering if we could meet someplace for a talk."

"Sure," I said, "I could come to your office—"

"I'd rather do it someplace else," he said. "I'm out and about. Anyplace you say is fine with me."

"Okay," I said. "Do you know where the Bourbon Street Blues and Boogie Bar is, in Printer's Alley?"

"Downtown," he said. "I'll find it."

"How about noon?"

"I'll be there."

I broke the connection.

"Sheldrake?" Nikki asked.

"The detective who talked to me yesterday at the Bannister house, about the blood in the pool."

"Does he know he's meetin' you downstairs from where you live?" she asked.

"No, but he said anyplace was okay with him."

"What's he want?" she asked.

"I don't know," I said. "He hasn't found Bannister or his daughter-in-law, yet. I guess he just has some more questions."

"Well," she said, "I'll leave you to it, then. I gotta go home. I'm workin' on some new songs. That is, if I can concentrate." She stood up. "Thanks for lettin' me crash, and the shirt." She touched Clapton's face, right between her pokey nipples. "Get it back to you when I can, nice and clean."

"No problem."

I started to get up, but she put her hand on my shoulder to stop me, leaned over and kissed my cheek.

"Talk to ya soon, Auggie."

"Hopefully, I said, "I'll have somethin' to tell you."

"Me, too."

She waved and went out the door.

CHAPTER 61

"BEER?" I asked. "Or is it too early?" I snapped my fingers. "Wait, you're on duty."

"Actually, I'm on my own time," he said, "and it's never too early."

I waved at the bartender, who came over.

"Whatever he's havin'," Sheldrake said.

"Fat Tire today," I said. It wasn't local, but it was good on draft.

"Fine."

The bartender brought two nice fresh ones over, and grabbed the one I had been working on, which still had about an inch in it.

"Thanks." I said. "So, Detective, what's up?"

"Tell me about Hammer Dylan," he said, after a sip of his beer.

"I thought you were off duty."

"I am," he said, "but I'd still like to know."

I hesitated, if I didn't know how much he already knew. Was he testing me? To see I'd lie?

"What do you want to know, exactly?"

"Is he alive?"

"What if he is."

"Then he's a person of interest in his agent's disappearance," Sheldrake said. "You'd have to tell me where he is."

"I don't know where he is," I said, truthfully. "The last place I saw him was . . . out there."

"At the Bannister house?"

"Yes."

"Who else was there?"

"Bannister One, Evangeline, his daughter-in-law," I told him, "and Bannister Three, his grandson."

"We spoke with young Mr. Bannister," Sheldrake said. "He told us the same things,. That was the last place he saw Hammer."

"Then you already knew that Hammer was alive when you asked me."

"Yes."

"And you wanted to see if I'd lie."

"Right."

"And I didn't."

"You . . . were evasive."

"No, I told you I saw him out there."

"After you evaded, first."

I decided to keep quiet.

"Oh, don't worry," he said. "You're not in any trouble. I was just wondering if you wanted to clarify anything, and maybe tell me where I could find Hammer Dylan—uh, for questioning."

"What did Carter Three say?"

"Carter Three?"

"It's just easier for me."

"What do you call the old man? Carter One?"

"Or the Original," I said. "So, uh, what did Three say?"

"He left his grandfather, his mother, and Hammer together at the house. Arguing."

"Do you believe him?"

"Should I?"

"Why not?"

"So that would mean something happened after he left. Maybe the arguing got violent. Somebody ended up bloody, and the blood got into the pool."

"And the other two took the third person to the hospital."

"Only thing is, we checked all the hospitals and walk-in clinics," Sheldrake said. "None of them were brought in."

"So we're back to square one," I said. "Something happened there, and we don't know when, or to who."

"Right." He finished his beer. "Thanks for the beer."

"That's it?"

"That's it." He got off his bar stool. "You can go back upstairs now."

"Upstairs?"

"Where you live." He pointed to the ceiling. "Upstairs?"

"Oh, yeah, well," I said, "this was just . . . convenient."

"You musicians," he said. "Funky place to live, funky lifestyle . . . you probably have a girl up there right now."

"No," I said, "no girl," but I didn't tell him I did about an hour ago.

As he walked out I found it interesting that he thought of me as a musician rather than a private detective. That meant he knew more about me than he was letting on.

―

I had another beer and was heading for my downstairs door when my cell phone rang.

"Yep?" I said.

"Auggie, it's Harley."

"Harley, man, are you all right. You sound—"

"—like shit, I know. That's how I feel. But I've got somethin' for you."

"What's that?"

"An address."

"Okay."

"You got a pen?"

"Yeah, wait." I went back into the Boogie, and asked the bartender for a pen and paper. "Okay, shoot."

He read it off to me.

"That doesn't sound familiar," I said. "Where is that?"

"It's in Anthem."

CHAPTER 62

ANTHEM.

It was the town I had gone to in order to check out that post office box, the one I'd had Jesse Fogarty sitting on to see who was collecting the mail there.

Driving to Anthem reminded me that I hadn't yet met Jesse to pay him for his stake-out duty at the post office. I'd have to take care of that soon. After all, Harley had told him he could trust me for the money.

It was about a three hour drive from Nashville, which gave me time to think about Hammer Dylan, Nikki Rialto, and the members of the Bannister family. I was dealing with two different situations—finding Hammer for Bannister Three, and finding Nikki for Hammer—both of which involved Hammer Dylan.

And then there was the murder, which I wasn't working on since it was an open police case, but which also involved Hammer. He was the link between all 3 of these events.

Although Anthem was a small river town along the Cumberland, I was going to need help finding the address Harley had given me on Alley Street. The post office or city hall seemed the best places for that. I decided on the post office, since I'd been there once before and knew where it was.

When I entered the same gray-haired, 50-ish man I'd spoken to the first time was there.

"Well, hello," he greeted. "Back again?"

"Don't you get a day off?" I asked.

"Not much chance of that," he said. "I'm the postmaster." He pointed to a framed certificate on the wall that said he was Dennis Fisher, Postmaster. "What can I do for you? Still looking for a P.O. box?"

"No," I said, "this time I'm looking for an address. One-oh-six Alley Street."

"Good thing you stopped in," he said. "You'd never find that on your own. There are only three houses on Alley Street. In fact, there aren't too many people in this town who even know it exists."

That's what made it perfect for Hammer Dylan.

I followed the postmaster's directions, and found Alley Street, which ran one block between two of Anthem's main streets, but was hidden from view by overgrown trees. The three houses there were very private residences, as a result.

When I drove up the street it started out paved, but quickly turned to a dirt road. On a slight incline, it must have been murder to drive up—or down--when it was raining and muddy. I passed two homes before I came to the one I wanted. They all looked as if they were meant to be summer or vacation homes.

The address 106 was a house up on a hill on about 3 acres of land, surrounded by trees. When I pulled up in front and stepped onto the porch, I saw a panoramic view of the Cumberland River down below. I took a few moments to stand at the rail and take it all in.

I knocked on the front door, got no answer. The front of the house was actually two big picture windows, but the curtains were drawn inside. The deck wrapped around the house, so I walked to the back and found another door. There was a small window, with a frilly curtain inside through which I could see a kitchen.

I knocked on the back door for a while, but got no answer. There was no other car in the driveway, and nothing behind the house.

I tried the door, found it locked. Then I went around to the front door and did the same thing with the same result.

I walked around the entire deck, then stepped down off of it and walked around the entire house. At one point I could see that someone had spread mothballs under the house, which I knew people did to drive snakes away.

Back on the deck I decided it was worth trying to force my way in, since I'd driven all that way. The kitchen door in the back seemed the most likely, so I went back there, started by pressing my shoulder to it to see if I could force it. Luckily, the lock on the door wasn't very good, and slipped with just a little pressure.

I entered the kitchen, closing the door behind me. There was a window over the sink, with plenty of light coming through. I searched there first, but didn't find much beyond some canned goods—vegetables, soup, beef stew—and nothing in the frig except for a couple of bottles of Fat Bottom Ruby red ale, and a container of spoiled milk. Under the counter was a garbage pail, lined with a black plastic bag, with empty cans and cereal boxes and Fat Bottom bottles inside.

There was a small bathroom between the kitchen and a laundry room. There was, however, no washer or dry attached to the pipes. The room was used mostly for storage —boxes, bags, buckets, mops, brooms, tools . . . I opened a couple of the boxes, found them filled with music sheets.

The house was small, but there was a level up and a level down. Down was a living room and dining room set-up, with a sofa, t.v., and dining room table.

I stopped in front of the small bathroom, then stepped inside. I wondered how anyone could move around in there without banging a knee, or their head, just by turning around.

I looked at myself in the mirror over the small sink, then opened it and found a variety of over-the-counter painkillers. When I looked into the sink I frowned, and leaned over. Faintly, I could see some red stains on the porcelain. The shower curtain was drawn, so I pulled it back and saw some bloodstained wet towels in the tub. Damn it, if this *was* Hammer's house, he had returned here either bleeding, or with blood on him. He had cleaned himself up, tried to clean the sink, but gave up when it came to these towels. Unless he meant to take care of them later.

Upstairs was the interesting part. It was all one room, but split by a closet. On one side was a bed, dresser and night table. The other side was set up like a small studio, with several guitars, amplifiers, headsets and microphones. Against one was a turntable, next to it a table with a stack of vinyl albums on it. There was not a computer anywhere in the house.

There was a metal music stand with some sheets on it— handwritten sheets. Somebody had been working on a song or, by the look of the number of sheets, an album. I leafed through the pages, found one that really interested me. At the top was written THE LAST SWEET SONG OF HAMMER DYLAN.

Bingo.

I no longer had any doubt that this was where Hammer Dylan had been living possibly for years. And he had returned here very recently.

It was at that point I heard the front door open, right below me. I could hear the jingle of keys, which meant that someone had used the key. Was it Hammer, or someone else looking for Hammer? Like cops. If it was cops I was going to have to explain what I was doing there.

There was a door leading from the bedroom to a small, upper deck. Briefly, I thought about going out that way and climbing down. But my car was in the driveway, so it was no secret I was there.

I decided to play it straight, and went down the steps to the second level, then looked to see who was there, on the first.

CHAPTER 63

"YOU ALWAYS BREAK into people's houses?"

I stared at Hammer, came down the stairs.

"Where the hell have you been?"

"Here," Hammer said, putting the two bags of groceries he was carrying down on the dining room table. "Why?"

"Well, first of all," I said, "you were supposed to meet me and Nikki at my place yesterday."

"I, uh, couldn't make it."

"You could've called."

"My phone died."

I couldn't say he was lying, because when I tried to call him his phone was out of service.

"Was she disappointed?" he asked.

"She was crushed," I said, "but then there's your agent, Carter the Original, and Vangie."

"Why? Did somethin' happen to them?"

"You tell me," I said. "I went there to see if they knew where you were. They're missing and there was blood in the pool."

"Omigod," he said. "What could've—"

"Don't even try it, Hammer," I said, cutting him off, impatiently. "I saw the bloody towels in the bathtub. What the hell happened there?"

He moved past me, picked up the bags of groceries and started up the stairs.

"You want a beer?" he asked.

"You got two left, so yeah," I said.

He got the Fat Bottoms out of the fridge and brought them back down.

"Have a seat," he said.

We sat at opposite ends of the old, beat-up couch and sipped our beer.

"Look." He held up his right hand, which had a bandage on it, holding his bottle in his left. "I cut my hands. That's where the blood came from on the towels. I just got back from the hospital in the next town, gettin' stitched up."

"So it didn't happen at Carter Bannister's house?" I asked. "That's not your blood at the edge of the pool, and floating in the water?"

"No," he said, "I don't know what happened at Carter's house. I hope they're all right."

"Well," I said, "the police want to talk to you about it? They're lookin' for you."

"Do they even know I'm alive?" he asked.

"They do."

"Shit."

"This place looks like you haven't been here for a while," I said.

"I haven't," he confirmed. "I been stayin' at a cheap motel near Nashville."

"Come on, Hammer," I said. "Talk to me. What happened yesterday? Why didn't you come and see Nikki?"

He looked away briefly, as if searching for the answer.

"You want the truth?"

"That would be a nice change."

He took a long drink before answering.

"I was scared."

"Of what?"

"Of what she might say," Hammer admitted. "Come on, Auggie, I ran out on the girl and her mother. At least, that's how she's gotta be thinkin'."

"You didn't know about her, Hammer," I said. "I mean, if you were telling me the truth about that part."

"I was," he said, "but . . . I was doin' a lot of drinkin' in those days. How many other girls do you think I got pregnant and never knew?"

"Well," I said, "right now you only have to deal with the one you know about."

"Yeah, I guess you're right." He took another drink. "You think she'll agree to meet me, again?"

"I can ask," I said. "I think she'll say yes."

"Okay," he said, "then set it up. I'll be there, this time . . . I swear!"

"Yeah, okay."

We both stood up.

"About your hand," I said. "Where did it happen?"

"Out in back of the house," he said. "I was actually sharpenin' the knife. I musta done a really good job."

"How do I get in touch with you?"

"I got a new phone."

He took it out and we punched the number into my phone.

"You're not gonna run out on me again, are you?" I asked. "Or Nikki?"

"No," he said. "I'll be there."

"And get rid of those bloody towels, just in case the cops come around to talk to you."

"Are you gonna tell 'em where I am?"

"I'm not gonna call 'em but if they ask I may have to, if I want to keep my license."

"Yeah," he said, sourly, "I can see that."

"You've got nothin' to hide, right?" I asked. "I mean, except for the fact that you haven't been dead all these years."

Before I left I walked around to the back of the house. I figured the spot where Hammer had been when he cut his hand should have some blood to mark it.

I looked all over the back, against the house, around the back deck, and on the grass, and I couldn't find blood, anywhere. If he had cut himself that seriously that he needed to go to the emergency room, surely there would be some sign of it.

He said he went to the hospital in the next town up. I got back in my car and drove.

CHAPTER 64

THE NEXT TOWN UP was called Valley View, and the hospital bore the same name. I went into the emergency room, and they had no record of anyone having their hand stitched in the past few hours. I had to slip the registration clerk $50 to get that much information.

Out in the parking lot I sat in my car for a few moments, wondering what my next move should be. Go back to Anthem and confront Hammer? It wasn't my job to discover what had happened at Carter Bannister's house. It was my job to find Hammer--which I did--and to put him together with Carter Three--which I did--and to put Nikki together with him—which I tried to do.

And still intended to do.

So I'd leave questioning Hammer about the Bannisters up to the police. All I had left to do was put Nikki and Hammer together.

I started the engine, pulled out of the parking lot and headed the car for Nashville.

On the way back I realized that the Bannister house was almost halfway between Nashville and Anthem. That meant Hammer only had about an hour and a half drive. He could have driven back from the house and washed the blood off when he got there. It would still have been wet.

Crap. I couldn't stop thinking about those bloody towels.

I put a CD in the player, tried to just concentrate on Rascal Flats and the road.

———

I was starving when I got home. I called Nikki to see if she was hungry. She said she was if I was willing to meet in half-an-hour at Robert's Western World on Broadway. Since it was practically around the corner, I said yes. I could wait that long to eat.

I had a quick beer down in the Boogie, listened to a bit of a local band's music, then left and walked right up to 4th Ave. I turned left and it was less than a three-block walk to Broadway.

Robert's has been described as "divey" which a lot of people like. Fried bologna sandwiches and affordable beer are the draw. And good music, but that was the draw up and down Broadway.

———

I entered under the huge lighted marquee that had "Robert's" in purple neon, and a big orange guitar underneath. Nikki had already gotten us a table in the crowded bar. She had a PBR in front of her. $2.50 Pabst Blue Ribbons were a specialty at Robert's.

I sat across from her.

A middle-aged waitress whose name I didn't remember smiled at me and said, "Ain't seen you here in a while, Auggie."

"That's because there's so many places in town to eat."

"Whataya have?"

I resisted the lure of the domestic beers and ordered a Yazoo Dos Perros.

"Sorry," she said, "I know you like locals, but I still got a taste for cheap beer. It comes from my upbringing."

"No problem," I said. "Did you order food?"

"Not yet," she said. "I showed *some* manners and decided to wait for you."

The waitress came back with my Yazoo and we ordered a fried bologna sandwich for Nikki, with fries. I ordered the boneless Pork Sandwich with sweet potato fries.

"Comin' up, darlin'," she said, before walking away.

"Darlin'?" Nikki said, with a grin. "Has she been up to your place?"

"No," I said, "she's just bein' friendly."

"Well," she said, "I happen to know you've got a thing for older women."

"Gimme a break," I said, but I returned her smile.

We both drank some beer and then she got serious.

"Did you find Hammer?"

"I did."

"Did he say why he didn't show up?"

I decided to be honest, and let Hammer deal with it.

"He said he was afraid."

"Afraid? Of what?"

"You."

"What the hell is there to be afraid of?"

"The way you might look at him, or talk to him," I said. "He figures you must think he deserted you and your mom."

"But I know he didn't," she said. "My mom never told him about me until recently."

"And why did she do that?"

"Why do you think?" Nikki asked. "Money."

"Well, she got some."

"Besides," she said, "she probably chased him away all those years ago. She could be a real bitch."

"Then?"

"And now."

The waitress came with our orders and we got busy. Eating at Robert's usually filled both hands, as well as your mouths and bellies.

———

After dinner we each had coffee and a Moon Pie, and then chased it all down with another beer.

"So where do we stand with Hammer?" she asked.

"He's gonna call."

"Really?"

"I think he will," I said. "I pretty much told him what you told me, that you wouldn't blame him."

"Well," she said, "you were right."

"So I think he'll call."

She raised her PBR bottle and we clinked.

———

I thought Nikki might ask to spend the night, and I wasn't sure what my answer would be, but when we walked outside she said, "Good-night, Auggie. Give me a call when you hear from him."

"I will," I promised.

During the walk home, the lights went out.

CHAPTER 65

I CAME TO SLOWLY. That's what happens when you get hit on the head.

Again.

I tried to touch my head, but my hands were bound. I looked around and realized I was in my own apartment.

"You don't keep much in your refrigerator," someone said.

I looked around, saw a man coming toward me, gnawing on a leftover chicken leg.

"And no stove? What's that about?" a second voice asked.

I turned my head painfully and saw the second man, sitting on the sofa. I squinted at hm. He was familiar.

"A microwave suits me fine," I said.

My head cleared slowly and I realized I was tied to a wooden chair that I used when I was working on my guitars.

"Why don't you guys take what you want and go?" I asked.

The two of them laughed. The one with the chicken

was in his 30s, the one on the sofa his 40s, not kids looking for money for a quick fix. But what were they looking for?

"You think we're here to rob you?" the first man asked, waving the chicken leg at me. "You think if we wanted to rob you on the street we woulda known where you live."

"You could've got my address from my wallet."

"We didn't bother with your wallet," the second one said. "We already knew where you live."

"Well, if not to rob me, then whataya want?" I asked.

Chicken Leg came and stood right in front of me. By now I realized my hands were tied behind me, and my legs were tied to the legs of the chair.

"Where's Hammer Dylan?" he asked.

"What? Hammer Dylan's been dead for years. Don't you know anythin' about country—"

He backhanded me across the face with his left hand. I felt my lip split, and licked the blood away.

"If there's one thing I hate," he said, "it's goddamned country music."

"Me, too," the second one said. "Too twangy. Too many damn guitars."

"Like those," the first man said, looking over my head at my guitars on their stands.

"What?"

"Earl, start on those guitars," the first man said. "Smash 'em one by one."

"Hey, Dave, you said no names," Earl bitched.

"Forget it!" Dave snapped. "Just do it."

"Yeah, yeah . . ."

"Hey, wait—" I started as Earl got up from the sofa. He had a grin on his face like a man who liked smashing things.

"You can stop this, friend," he said. "Just tell us where Hammer Dylan is."

"But . . . why?"

"Uh, so we don't smash your guitars to bits," Earl said, from behind me.

"Or your head," Dave said.

"No, I mean, why do you need to find Hammer Dylan?" I asked. "Who put you up to this?"

"Whataya mean?"

"And who told you where I was?" I asked. "I mean, you must've known I'd be walkin' back here, in order for you to be waitin' on the street for me."

"Look," Dave said, "we're askin' the questions." He looked over my head. "Earl? Start with that red one."

The red one was an Electric Rickenbacker I had just gotten. It had been played by Roger McGuinn of The Byrds.

"Okay, okay, hold on," I said, cringing against the coming sound of a guitar being smashed.

"You ready to talk?" Dave asked.

"Sure," I said, "but look, my hands are going numb. Can you loosen these ropes?" I was just killing time.

"Yeah, okay," Dave said, looking at Earl. "Do it." He stepped back, dropped the naked chicken leg onto the coffee table and licked his fingers clean.

Good. If Earl was loosening my ropes, then he wasn't destroying a priceless guitar.

I had no idea what would come next.

Then my door slammed open.

CHAPTER 66

THE THREE OF US—DAVE, Earl and me—were surprised when my door was kicked open and cops came pouring in. Both men put their hands up and surrendered immediately. Hollinger followed the uniforms in, untied me, and walked me outside. Now we watched as they loaded the two men into the back of a police van.

"Sure you don't need to go to the hospital?" Detective Hollinger asked me.

"No," I said. "I've just got a split lip and a bump on the head."

"What'd they want?" Hollinger asked. "Money? How'd they get in?"

"They grabbed me off the street," I said. "Knocked me out, used my key to open the door and get in. Then I guess they tied me to the chair and waited for me to wake up."

"And?"

"They wanted to know where Hammer Dylan is."

"Why would they want to know that?" he asked.

"I don't know," I said. "I told them he was dead, but they didn't believe me."

"That's how you got the split lip?"

"Yeah, but that didn't do it," I said. "They threatened to smash my guitars, starting with the Rickenbacker."

"A what?"

"The red one. Roger McGuinn played it." He stared at me. "He was with the Byrds."

"I know who the Byrds were. Must be worth a fortune."

"To me it's priceless."

"So you were going to tell them where Hammer Dylan is?" Hollinger asked.

"I don't know."

"Are you going to tell *me* where he is?"

"Why do you need to know?"

"Just to ask him some questions."

"What if I told you he's dead, as far as I know?"

"Is he?"

"He could be."

"Velez, do you know where he is?"

"No."

"What do you want to do about these two guys?"

"Charge them," I said. "Find out who they work for."

"You don't know who sent them after you?"

"No."

"Okay," Hollinger said. "I'll have a talk with them."

"Let me know what you find out."

"Right." He started to walk away, then turned back. "I heard from Detective Sheldrake. He's looking for Hammer Dylan, too. I'd think long and hard about this, Auggie."

"Yeah, thanks. I will."

As he walked away I thought, I'd told him the truth, I didn't know who sent those two guys after me.

But I had an idea.

It was Earl. I now remembered where I had seen him before.

CHAPTER 67

THE NEXT MORNING I had a headache, but it wasn't something I couldn't live with.

Dave and Earl had been right about one thing. I had no food in the house, so I went to the Back Alley Diner on Arcade for a good breakfast.

I went over what had happened the night before, and what it meant that one of the men who attacked me was Earl—the Earl I'd seen in Lisa Martin's house in Tulsa, Oklahoma. Earl was wrapped firmly around Lisa's little finger, so for him to be here looking for Hammer Dylan, she must've sent him and his buddy, Dave. The question was, since Lisa was Nikki's mother, did Nikki know? The only way the two men could've been waiting for me on the street was if Nikki had called them as soon as we split up in front of Robert's. I was starting to think that mother and daughter were looking for Hammer Dylan for totally different reasons than I'd been given—and I was being used.

I hadn't finished by ham-and-eggs yet, but I took out my cell and tried the number Hammer had given me, hoping it was working.

"Auggie?"

"Yeah, Hammer," I said. "I'm glad you picked up."

"I told you I would," he said. "Look, I can see Nikki today—"

"That's what I called you about," I said. "Let's hold off on that."

"But why?"

I told him what happened to me the night before.

"What's that got to do with Nikki and me?" Hammer asked.

"One of the guys was named Earl," I said. "I saw him with Lisa Martin in Tulsa. He's her boyfriend."

"What?"

"I'm thinking she sent him to find you."

"But I paid her."

"I know that," I said. "I'm thinking maybe that was a smokescreen."

"For what?"

"I don't know," I said. "There's got to be another reason they want to find you."

"And what about Nikki?"

"Maybe she's got nothing to do with whatever her mother and Earl are doing. But I was with her last night, and on my way home I get jumped. Is that a coincidence?"

"You think she sent 'em?"

"I think she could've made a call, telling them I was walking home."

"I don't get any of this."

"Look," I said, "the man who was killed at your tribute might've been killed because somebody thought he was you."

"And what about the Axe Man?"

"He might have been killed because he wouldn't tell where you were."

"So where's this Earl asshole now?"

"He and his buddy are in custody," I said. "Maybe the cops will get him to admit who he's working for, or with, and why."

"So you want me to stay away from Nikki for how long?" Hammer asked.

"Until I find out what's actually going on," I said.

"And how are you gonna do that?"

"Easy," I said. "I'm gonna ask her."

"When?"

"Sometime today," I said. "Let's hope between the cops questioning Earl and me talking to Nikki, we know something by tomorrow."

"Okay," Hammer said, "I'll wait. But, by the way, what've you heard about Carter and Vangie?"

"Nothing," I said, "but I expect to hear from Detective Sheldrake real soon." It seemed like Hollinger and Sheldrake might be coordinating their efforts.

I thought about asking him about the cut on his hand and the bloody towels, but I decided that was Sheldrake's business. My concern was being used by Nikki and her mother. I didn't like being anyone's bird dog.

"Okay," Hammer said, "I guess it's a good thing I did some shoppin'. Only I shoulda bought some booze."

"Hopefully," I said, "this won't take long, Hammer. You can keep workin' on your sweet song."

"My last sweet song," he said. "You saw that, huh? You know, I could use some help on it. A good guitar player, a good lyricist. You know anybody?"

My heart started beating faster, thinking he might be talking about *nm*, but I said, "I'll give it some thought."

CHAPTER 68

I CALLED Nikki to arrange a meet with her.

"You've got news so soon?" she asked.

"I do, but I don't want to share it over the phone."

"Where do you want to meet?"

I thought somewhere out in the open would work best, so I said, "Bradley Park."

"Near Music Row," she said. "Okay."

Bradley was a famous Nashville performer and songwriter, who later became a publisher.

"Meet next to the statue of him sittin' at the piano."

"Suits me. In an hour?"

"That's good."

"See you there."

Dave and Earl wouldn't be out of custody in an hour. I wondered if she could recruit any other strong-arm help by that time.

I didn't have a gun, but then Earl and Dave hadn't been armed, either. They were just going to bust me or my guitars up. And if Nikki didn't have time to get more help, I'd just be dealing with her—or her and her mother.

I decided I didn't need a weapon to meet Nikki in Bradley Park—but I did decide to get there ahead of her.

——

I was sitting on the bench near old Bradley when she entered the park and walked over to me. Several men had passed me, in either direction, and a couple of women had looked me over. One, with a baby stroller, saw me and increased her pace. An older woman with an overcoat stumbled by, huddled like she was cold, sparse brown hair shot with grey.

"Sit," I said.

She looked around.

"Your guys aren't comin'," I said. "Dave and your mom's boyfriend, Earl?"

She looked at me and frowned.

"What?"

"They're in jail."

She sat down.

"Are you gonna deny you made a phone call last night after we left Robert's?"

She didn't answer, kept looking down.

"I can check your cell for outgoing calls."

She looked at me, reached into her pocket.

"Don't give it to him, Bright," a woman's voice said from behind us.

Nikki's temper flared.

"Don't call me that!"

"All right, all right," the woman said. "Taylor."

"It's Nikki, now."

"Oh, you and all your names."

The woman moved around to stand in front of us. It was

the older woman in the beat-up coat. Without make-up Lisa Martin looked years older, with wrinkles, and I swore no teeth.

"Lisa?"

She smiled, revealing some bottom teeth, but none on top.

"I know," she said, "without my dentures and wig it's a shock, huh? But I still got the tattoo on my fine butt. Wanna see?"

"No, thanks," I said. "I'll take your word for it."

"Momma," Nikki said, "I coulda handled this."

"I don't think so, Taylor. I think you kinda got a hankerin' for this fella. Not that I blame ya. He looks like pretty good rough trade to me."

I'd been called a lot of things in my life, but rough trade?

"All right, ladies," I said. "Earl and Dave are in jail. They're gonna give you up, so where do we go from here?"

"Nobody cares about Earl and his pal," Lisa said. "And from here you're gonna take us to Hammer."

"Why would I do that?"

"Because if ya don't," Lisa said, bringing a hand out of her pocket, "I'll put a bullet in ya."

She was holding a revolver, looked like a .38 to my untrained eye. In Afghanistan, we didn't carry revolvers, so I didn't have much experience with them.

"And what are you gonna do if I drive you to him?" I asked.

"I'm gonna put a bullet in him," Lisa said.

"Why?" I asked. "You got your money."

"I haven't got what I really want," Lisa said, "and neither has my daughter."

She was holding the gun close to her body, so that the

coat hid it from view. People passing weren't able to tell what was happening.

"And what's that?"

"I told you," Lisa sad. "To put a bullet into Hammer Dylan where it'll do the most damage."

I looked at Nikki.

"Has that been the plan all along?" I asked.

Nikki didn't answer.

"Yes," Lisa said, "it has. Her coming here to Nashville, her success, it was all to try and find her father—the man who ruined our lives."

"And what about Hoyt Bennett?" I asked.

"Who the hell is that?" Lisa asked.

"The Axe Man," I said.

"The man with the music store, Mama," Nikki said.

"Oh, that was those idiots, Earl and Dave. They asked him where Hammer was and when he wouldn't answer they got carried away. They do like to smash things. After that I got mad and made them come home. But then you show up in Tulsa, so I hadda send them out here, again."

"Why not send them after me there?" I asked.

"I was gonna, but we couldn't find stupid Dave, that day."

"And what about the guy who was stabbed at Hammer's tribute show?" I asked.

"I don't know nothin' about that," Lisa said.

"The police still think Nikki did it."

"That's ridiculous," Lisa said. Nikki didn't say a word.

"And Carter Bannister and his daughter-in-law?" I asked. "Whose blood ended up in their pool?"

"I don't know anythin' about that, either," Lisa said, and then turned to her daughter. "Bri—I mean, Nikki, we've gotta get off the street. Where can we take this handsome young man so I can shoot him?"

I knew if I let them take me anywhere there was a good chance this crazy woman would shoot me. I had to stand my ground, and look casual about it. I crossed my legs and spread my arms across the back of the bench.

"I'm not tellin' you where he is," I said, "so you're gonna have to shoot me right here."

"You think I won't?" she asked.

"What would be the point?" I asked. "Dead I can't tell you a thing."

"But ya'll are sayin' you won't tell us," she pointed out. "I might as well shoot you right here."

"Go ahead," I said, my stomach clenching. "There are plenty of witnesses walking through the park."

"Nobody's gonna recognize me in this get-up," she said.

"They'll recognize Nikki," I said, "and she's already on the hook for one murder."

"She didn't do it!"

"She's gotta prove that," I said. "Meanwhile, you shoot me out here in the open, you'll be arrested in minutes. I called the police before I came here."

A look passed between them.

"You're a liar!" Lisa said.

"Why don't you sit on this bench with Nikki and me, Lisa, and we'll just wait."

She looked around, flexing her fingers on the gun nervously.

"Auggie," Nikki said, "she's gettin' ready to shoot you. You gotta tell us where he is."

"Wait a minute," I said, "who hit me over the head in an alley the other night. Was that Earl?"

Lisa rolled her eyes.

"That man does make stupid decisions on his own," she said. "There wasn't no point to that."

Now I wished I'd gotten a shot of my own in at Earl before Hollinger hauled him away. Maybe just a kick in the balls.

Lisa looked around again.

"So where are your cops, Auggie?" she asked me, getting more confident. My other problem was that suddenly, the park was empty.

Where had all the people gone?

CHAPTER 69

I WAS SCARED SHITLESS.

Of all the times for there to be no tourists walking around.

"Nervous, Auggie?" Lisa asked.

"Not me," I lied, looking at Nikki. "I think Nikki's the nervous one. If she didn't kill the man the cops think she did, then she's not going to want to be involved in murdering me, is she?"

Lisa looked at Nikki, who looked away.

"And what about you, Lisa?" I asked. "When's the last time you killed somebody?"

"Never," she said. "I been savin' it for Hammer Dylan. See, I never thought he was dead. The coward just went into hidin'."

"From you?"

"It don't matter what from," she said. "Probably from success. He's just a coward."

"What makes you say that?" I wanted to keep her talking. If she was talking, she wasn't shooting.

"Are you kiddin'?" she asked. "The night we was together, he cried. The man cried! Men ain't supposed to cry."

Well, I didn't know if Hammer was actually hiding out from success, but I didn't think crying made him a coward.

"Ya'll're makin' me lose my patience, Auggie," Lisa said.

I looked around. Still nobody in the park, or on the street.

And then I got it.

I looked around and spotted what I was hoping for. A flash of red.

"Lisa," I said, "if I was you I'd put that gun down and step away from it."

"You would? Why would you do that?"

"So you don't get shot."

Nikki looked at me, confused.

"Nikki,' I said, "go around behind your mom and tell her if there's a red laser sight on her back—but don't get in the way. Just tell her."

Hesitantly, Nikki got off the bench and walked over to her mom. She leaned over to look at her back.

"Oh, God," she said, "Mama, he's right."

"Ya'll are lyin'," Lisa said. "Why you sidin' with him, Bright, against your own Mama?"

"She's not, Lisa," I said. "Just turn around and you'll see the red laser sight on your chest."

She frowned at me, then slowly turned around, until her back was to me. I knew she could see the red dot on her chest, now, but I didn't know how she would react, and I didn't want her getting shot. So as soon as her back was turned I pushed myself off the bench and tackled her around the waist, taking her down to the ground.

The air went out of her and the gun fell from her hand. I picked it up, got to my feet and waved. I didn't know who I was waving to, or where they were, but the red dot of the laser sight vanished.

CHAPTER 70

"WHAT WERE YOU THINKING?" Detective Hollinger said. "We had her in our sights."

"That's what I was thinking," I told him. "I didn't want you to kill her."

"Then why'd you call me before you went to meet with Nikki?" he asked.

"I wasn't sure she'd come alone," I said. "After all, she did send Earl and Dave after me."

I looked over to where Lisa and Nikki were being led away in handcuffs. The park was now full of people, but they were mostly cops, or technicians associated with cops. Apparently they all came out when an armed suspect was involved.

"I wasn't sure if she was working alone, but I didn't really expect it to be her Mother. Well, yeah, I did, after I saw Earl."

"Right now we've got Lisa Martin on a gun charge," Hollinger said. "Maybe even attempted murder on you. That'll be up to the D.A.."

"What about Earl and Dave?" I asked. "Can you get them for killin' Hoyt Bennett and wrecking the Axe Man?"

"They haven't confessed yet," Hollinger said, "but I'll try playing the girls off the boys and see what I can come up with."

"And the dead guy from The Bluebird?"

"Sorry, Auggie, but I thought all along that Nikki did it."

"I guess that's between you, the D.A. and her lawyer, now."

"You're out?"

"I'm definitely out," I said.

"And what about Hammer Dylan?" Hollinger asked. "Is he going to stay dead?"

"I don't know," I said. "I guess I'll have to ask him."

"Well, come on down to the shop before you do that," Hollinger said. "We'll need a statement."

"You got it."

He turned and joined the parade of police personnel who were now leaving the park. Soon it would be open to the public, again.

—

After I made my statement I went to Hollinger's desk and Sheldrake was in his visitor's chair.

"What brings you here?" I asked.

"Hollinger and I have been working our cases together, figuring they might be connected."

"Cases?"

"I still haven't found Bannister or his daughter-in-law," Sheldrake said. "I'm hoping these two women might have somethin' to say about it."

"I don't think they do," I said.

"Why?"

"I don't think they had anything to do with what happened out there."

"Then who does?" Bannister asked.

"I have two guesses," I said.

"Hammer Dylan one of them?" Hollinger asked.

"Maybe."

"And who's the other one?" Sheldrake asked.

"Come with me," I said, "and we can all ask him."

━━

As we entered the office of the Bannister Agency, Nancy looked up from her desk in surprise.

"Auggie!"

"Nancy," I said, "meet Detectives Hollinger and Sheldrake. They want to talk to Carter. Is he here?"

"Um, he's not," she said. "In fact, I was about to close the office—"

"Mind if we take a look around?" Hollinger asked.

"Don't you need a warrant, or something?" Nancy asked.

"No," Sheldrake said.

They went into Carter Three's office, and I followed. Hollinger checked his desk, Sheldrake his bathroom.

"Look what I got," Sheldrake said. He came out holding a towel with blood on it.

"Nancy!" I called.

She came running in.

"When did they leave?" I asked.

"Auggie—"

"Don't bother lying, Nancy," I said. "We've got the

bloody towel. When did they leave, and where did they go?"

She hesitated, then answered.

Bannister Three's apartment was in Germantown. Nancy told us he had his grandfather and mother there.

"What was he doing with them?" I asked.

"Yelling, mostly."

"About what?"

"I don't know," she said. "I just figured it was family stuff."

"What about the blood?"

"What blood?" She looked honesty puzzled.

Hollinger arranged for an officer to take her home. Actually, what he was doing was making sure she didn't call her boss and warn him that we were on our way.

"I rode with Hollinger, while Sheldrake drove with two uniformed cops. We parked down the street from Bannister Three's address and walked. When we reached the door we were about to ring the bell when we heard shouting from inside.

"Sounds like a call for help, don't you think?" Hollinger asked.

"I do," Sheldrake said.

They both drew their guns, Hollinger kicked the door open and they went in together. Feeling left out, I followed.

"What the hell—" Bannister Three shouted.

"We heard someone shouting," Hollinger said. "Thought there might be trouble."

The 4 of us looked over at Bannister the Original, sitting

on the sofa, wearing a blood-stained shirt. Vangie was seated next to him, looking lost.

"Well, well," I said. "Trouble in the family?"

CHAPTER 71

WE ALL WENT to Hollinger's shop. Bannister One and Vangie were put in one interrogation room, while Bannister Three was in another. Because the blood had been found in Bannister the Original's house, Sheldrake was questioning them.

With Bannister Three having hired me to find Hammer Dylan in the first place, Hollinger was questioning him. He allowed me to sit in, on the condition I keep my trap shut . . .

"What'd you do to your grandfather?" Hollinger asked.

"Why don't you ask me what he did to me?" Carter Three asked.

"We'll get to that," Hollinger promised. "Why don't you answer my question, first?"

"I didn't do anything to him," Carter Three insisted, with his arms folded.

"He's got a pretty bad cut on his head," Hollinger said "one that left some blood by and in the pool."

"I don't know anything about that," Carter Three insisted.

"Okay," Hollinger said, "that's not my case, anyway. I'll let Detective Sheldrake talk to you about that. Let's go back to when you hired Auggie Velez to find Hammer Dylan. How did you know Dylan was still alive?"

"I suspected it because of things that were said between my grandfather and mother as I was growing up."

"And what was that?"

"It wasn't exactly what was said, but how," Carter Three said.

"What do you mean?"

"They never talked about him like he was dead," he said. "In the beginning I was too young to notice, but as I got older I started to realize, they weren't talking about a dead man."

"I see. So that's why you wanted to start up the agency, again?" Hollinger asked.

"Right," Carter Three said, "I figured I'd have a head start if I could find Hammer. So I hired Auggie."

"Why not just ask your grandfather and mother where he was?" Hollinger asked.

"I did," Carter Three said. "When I asked them to let me re-open the agency they said sure, why not? Have a go at it. But when I asked about Hammer, they clammed up. *That's* when they started acting like he was dead, but by then it was too late. I knew."

"And?"

"*And* I asked them about it, *and* they wouldn't admit that he was alive. But they told me to go ahead and try to make a go of the agency."

"But without Hammer . . ." I said, speaking for the first time. Hollinger decided to let it go.

Carter One looked at me.

"Without Hammer, I've got nothin'!" he snapped.

Hollinger stared at me, so I figured I had the go ahead.

"But once I found him?" I asked. "What then?"

"If I could get him to do a new album," Carter Three said, "the sky was the limit!"

I looked at Hollinger. We both had the same thought. That was a motive to keep him alive, not kill him.

"Let's step outside," Hollinger suggested.

In the hall I said what I was thinking and he agreed.

"What about the dead guy at The Bluebird?" I asked. "Any i.d. yet?"

"Nothing," Hollinger said. "But I'm still thinking Nikki killed him, thinking he was her dad, and the two lugs who grabbed you killed the Axe Man. So, my cases are solved."

"If nobody confesses—" I started.

"—it's up to the D.A. to prove it to a jury in court."

"And what about Sheldrake's case?"

"That's his problem," Hollinger said. "I've got my own caseload to think about."

"So what about Carter Three, in there?"

"I'm going to leave him there," he said. "Sheldrake wants to talk to him. But I don't even know if he has a case."

"I guess that'll depend on what Carter the Original tells him," I said.

"Hang around and find out, if you want," he said. "I'm going to be booking the others."

"What about Lisa?"

"I'll talk to the D.A. and see what we can charge her with," he said. "But she might get out on bail if all we've got is today's gun charge."

"But if her guys killed Hoyt Bennett—"

"If she wasn't there, I might be able to get her for

conspiracy to commit—but again, that's up to the District Attorney."

He walked away, leaving me in the hall. The question that was left was, how did Carter the Original's blood end up in the pool? An accident, or an assault?

———

Sheldrake didn't let me sit in like Hollinger had. And he didn't allow me to watch from the other side of a two-way mirror, like on t.v.. So I simply had to wait in the hall for him to come and say to me, "Accident."

"What?"

"He slipped and fell."

"Says who?"

"Everybody," Sheldrake said. "Him, his daughter-in-law and his grandson."

"They all tell the same story?"

"Yes."

"But you checked hospitals, walk-in clinics, didn't find him."

"He skipped through the cracks."

"So who treated him?"

"I don't care."

"And what about Hammer Dylan?"

"I haven't spoken to him," Sheldrake said.

"Don't you think you should?"

"No," he said, "I have three people tellin' me the same story. Family members, by the way."

"Yeah, a dysfunctional family."

"Not my problem."

I wondered what he would've said if I told him about the bloody towels at Hammer's house.

"Anythin' else?" he asked.

"No."

"Then case closed. Thanks for your help."

He took off down the hall. I left the building and went home.

CHAPTER 72

I DROVE my car up the alley to Hammer Dylan's house, hoping I'd find him there. I didn't have to worry. He was sitting on the deck, looking at the river and drinking a beer.

"Hey!" he called out, raising the bottle. "Beer?"

"Sure, why not?"

I sat across from him, thinking he was going to go inside to get me one, but he didn't move.

"What brings you up this way?"

"A bloody towel."

He frowned at me.

"I told you about that. I cut my hand."

"Yeah, and old Carter fell down, hit his head and bled into his pool."

"That's what I heard."

"But it's not what you saw, is it?"

"I heard it was case closed," Hammer said.

"I thought you offered me a beer."

"Here ya go!"

Lisa came out of the house, wearing tight shorts and t-shirt, so that the size of her implants and nipples were on full display.

"Thanks."

She nodded, smiled, leaned down and kissed Hammer, and then went back inside.

"What the hell is she doing here?" I asked him, keeping my voice down.

"She's out on bail," he said. "In fact, I bailed her out."

"But . . . why?"

"Our daughter's going to go on trial for murder," he said. "We've put our differences aside for her benefit."

I stared at him for a few seconds.

"That was very good," I said. "How long did it take you to memorize it?"

"Look, Auggie—"

"Hammer," I said, "I'm convinced that Lisa and Nikki were lookin' for you to kill you. And I almost helped 'em."

"We've put all that behind us," Hammer said. "Now it's about Bright."

"Nikki?"

"Bright's her real name."

"Hammer—"

"I've gotta thank you, Auggie. You're the one who brought us together as a family."

"You're a crazy man!" I said. "They might kill you in your sleep one day."

"Haven't you heard?" he asked, spreading his arms. "Hammer Dylan's been dead for years."

I drank half the beer, set the bottle down and stood up to leave.

"One more thing, Auggie," Hammer said.

"What's that?"

"I need your help."

"Who do you need found now?" I asked.

"No, not as a detective," he said. "As a song writer, and a guitar player."

"You're kiddin'."

He looked up at me with a serious expression. More serious than I'd ever seen.

"I've hit the wall with 'the Last Sweet Song of Hammer Dylan,'" he said. "Will ya help me?"

I took a few beats, then sat back down and picked up my beer.

A LOOK AT THE EYE IN THE RING

Miles Jacoby is torn between a career in the ring and his new ticket as a private investigator. When his sleuth mentor is murdered, it's bad enough that Miles's brother is charged. Worse, Miles finds himself in love with his brother's wife.

Said Elmore Leonard: *"If Eye in the Ring moved any faster you'd have to nail it down to read it."*

AVAILABLE NOW

BOOKS BY ROBERT J. RANDISI

Miles Jacoby Novels

Eye in the Ring

Beaten to a Pulp

Full Contact

Separate Cases

Hard Look

Stand-Up

Nashville P.I. Series

Honky Tonk Big Hoss Boogie

The Las Sweet Song of Hammer Dylan

In Collaboration with Christine Matthews

Murder Is the Deal of the Day

The Masks of Auntie Laveau

Same Time, Same Murder

ABOUT THE AUTHOR

Randisi was born and raised in Brooklyn, N.Y., and from 1973 through 1981 he was a civilian employee of the New York City Police Department, working out of the 67th Precinct in Brooklyn. After 41 years in N.Y, he now resides in Laughlin, NV, 90 miles South of Las Vegas, on the Colorado River, with his 25-year partner-in-life-and-crime, Marthayn Pelegrimas.

He is the author of the "Miles Jacoby," "Nick Delvecchio," "Joe Keough," and "Dennis McQueen," mystery series, and the co-author of the "Gil & Claire Hunt" series. He has been nominated four times for the Shamus Award from the Private Eye Writers of America, in the Novel and Short Story categories.